THE MAGISTER'S CHILD

SAMANTHA JACOBEY

Lavish Publishing LLC

Unexpected Magic #5

First Edition

All Rights Reserved

Published in the United States by Lavish Publishing, LLC, Midland, Texas

Paperback edition

ISBN: Paperback

Cover Design by: Victor R. Sosa

Cover Images: Canstock

www.LavishPublishing.com

Prologue

HUBERT WHISTLED LIGHTLY as he parked his car and strolled up to the prison. He didn't feel like he needed Morcant anymore, but he did owe him a final visit. A fond farewell, by all accounts.

Making his way through processing, he wore a lopsided grin. With pep in his step, he followed Jason down the corridor to the visitation chamber.

"You seem in a good mood," the guard observed casually.

"Yeah. I guess I am." Bert wiggled his fingers, a tingle of excitement running through him. "This will likely be the last visit I make. I'm going to miss talking to the old codger." He laughed at his inside joke.

Jason only shook his head, opening the door and letting him inside. "You know the drill."

"Yup." Bert bounced between the chairs, tossing imaginary hoop shots at the walls. Selecting a seat, he plunked down, casually draping an arm over the back of the chair while he waited for his magister to appear. When two more guards delivered the prisoner, he grinned.

"The news must be excellent today," Morcant observed

when he arrived at the table. "I've never seen you this giddy." Taking an empty seat, he faced his servant and waited.

"Well, I guess that it is." Hubert slapped the table, tilting towards him. "I got a new girl," he whispered with glee. "She's fabulous. And she works at that shop with your brother. So, things are pretty patched up between Joseline and me." He leaned back, beaming.

"Oh, that's wonderful news." The smile on Morcant's face sent a chill down the other man's spine. "What's her name?" he prodded.

Staring at him, Bert hated when Morcant was calm, like a cat waiting to pounce. "Hannah," he provided, a little less jovially. "She's Madam Demore's great niece."

"Hannah! How delightful. Finally grown up, then?"

"Yeah. She just graduated from college a few months ago." Hubert fidgeted with his fingers, suddenly regretting mentioning her at all. "Look, I needed to warn you that I may not be back over here for a while. We're pretty busy at the shop now that everything is opening back up and I'm not sure when I'll be able to get away."

"Oh, I'm sure you'll make it by," Morcant countered. "And I have a splendid idea. Let's induct Hannah into our new coven, shall we?"

Hubert blinked at him, opening his palm. "Sure. I guess we can do that," he offered, not really seeing how. "But... you're in here. Is there a way to do it without you?"

"Oh, don't worry. I'll take care of that." Morcant leered at him, his lips drawn into a tight smirk. "Now, how are things going with my brother?" The grin disappeared as he stared at him. "Or were you not part of the group in Virginia?" he growled, his voice deepening.

His jaw dropped and Bert cleared his throat. "No. Actually, Hannah and I have had quite a holiday since they've been gone. Blake had more renovations done on the shop, which have taken a whole month," he explained anxiously. "They won't be reopening until the group gets back, which should be any day now."

"I see." Morcant tapped the flat surface between them. "I guess it never occurred to you the renovations were a cover for what took place in another state?"

"Well, it wouldn't matter." Bert shrugged, growing weary of the conversation. "I wasn't invited. Oh, but Meri's father died while they were there. That could be why they haven't come back yet."

"Yes, I'm aware of Garrett's passing." Morcant sneered, driving Hubert to his feet.

Pushing the chair away from the table, Bert waved at the guard. "Listen, I gotta go. But I'll work on getting Hannah into the coven for you. I'll let you know how it goes in a few weeks, or so." Walking away, he left the old witch seated at the table with no plans to ever return.

ONE

The Store

"OH MY GOSH, THIS IS WONDERFUL!" Hannah praised, admiring Meri's choice of fabric for the chairs.

"Isn't it! I've sure missed this." The older girl beamed with pride. "You know, I went to a school in California for my degree. Then I moved to New York because I wanted my own shop one day, but it didn't work out for me." Meri sniffed, taken down a little at the realization of what she had yet to accomplish. "When I moved to New Orleans with Rider, we had big plans for my company, almost like a second try, but COVID really put a stop to all of it." She grinned at a random thought. "Maybe the third time will be the charm. If I can save enough doing this to get my start."

"Oh, Meri, you'll have enough, I'm sure! You've hit bad luck a few times, but you only fail if you quit trying." Hannah glanced at Sarah and Karen, who were applying the new cloth to the seats of the chairs Joseline had sanded down and refinished. "Your work shows too much promise for quitting."

Jos joined them, bringing in the last of the frames. "I have to agree on both counts. All this reclaimed furniture will be great, and this is only a taste of what my little sister can do."

"Thanks, Sis." Meri smiled up at her. "Will we have the tables by this afternoon?"

Joseline nodded, searching for her water bottle. "Yeah. They need another coat, which I'm on next. They'll be ready to move once they are past the tacky stage. Provided you're careful."

"Don't worry, we will be," Karen promised, admiring her girlfriend's work. "Our coffee shop is going to be totally unique."

"A wonderful place to relax and in a great location for those who want the unusual experience," Sarah agreed, happy to see the group getting along so well. "I just hope we have it all finished. Blake wants to do that grand reopening next week."

"We'll make it," Hannah assured. "Many hands make for light work."

"Amen to that," Joseline agreed, turning to head back outside.

"Good news, ladies," Blake sang, entering through the glass door and locking it behind him. Placing a basket on the counter, he pulled back the cover. "Fresh pastry anyone?"

"Like we're gonna say no," Sarah teased. Getting to her feet, she peered at the selection. "These look wonderful, honey. How much are they going to cost us?"

"With equipment and supplies, these will be almost half what I priced for us to make them ourselves," he boasted. "The baker down the street was more than happy to strike a deal. We are contracted to purchase a thousand units a week, and we get them for twenty cents apiece, with the option for more at that price when we need them. Our markup will be around eighty percent per bun."

"Wow. Do you think we'll sell that many?" Karen gasped. "It sounds like we'll be eating a lot of croissants."

"We may eat a few at the beginning, but once we get established, I think it will take off. Besides, the coffee has an even bigger markup, and it's the pairing that will make the most in sales," he explained. Selecting a jelly filled, he tore it in half. "I'm pretty proud of the arrangement."

"We can tell," Merideth agreed.

"Hey, are you saving any of those for me?" Rider quipped, joining them from the basement.

Avoiding his gaze, Meri quickly excused herself. "I need to visit the lady's room," she called, exiting swiftly.

"Still not speaking to me," Rider lamented, looking down at the box and no longer in the mood.

"Give her time," Sarah consoled. "She said you guys will always be friends."

"And you are both Josee's siblings. It's not like she can ever really get away from you," Karen pointed out.

"Thanks. That makes it so much better," Rider snapped. Snatching up a plain glazed, he glanced at the pots. "What, no coffee?"

"No, we haven't turned them on yet. Once we get the seating area finished, we'll give them a test run," Hanna explained.

"Well, that's fine. I have the one downstairs." He moped on his way back to the dungeon, where a seemingly endless stack of tomes awaited him.

"Poor guy," Hannah observed when he had dropped out of range. "He's pretty broken up that Merideth won't make up with him."

"It's his own fault," Blake spat tartly. "I warned him not to be a hero. Meri totally wants to be her own person, but he just kept pushing her."

"Still, she's pretty broken up about it as well," Sarah

pointed out. Seeing the other woman exit the toilet, she sighed. "She's just better at hiding it."

"Yeah," Blake agreed, watching Merideth pick her way through the comfy setting in the center of the sales floor. When she was closer, he called, "Hey, Meri! Remember when you thought my brother's table was creepy?"

Merideth giggled. "Yes. What made you think of that?"

"I noticed you still avoid touching it," he pointed out, coughing a sharp laugh.

"Yes. Well, it still freaks me out a little." She grinned at him, thankful for the distraction.

"Ok, ladies. I'm going to get some work done in the new office." Blake winked at her. "You girls have fun."

Hours later, the group gathered around to admire their handiwork. "This place is amazing," Sarah breathed. "I don't think I could be more pleased with it."

"I'll be pleased when it makes some money," Blake kidded. "Have we tried the coffee?"

"You go first," Merideth suggested, raising a hand towards the freshly brewed pots.

What's this one?" he asked, pointing at the third carafe that had no label.

"Hazelnut," Karen said shyly. "We bought a variety pack, so maybe we can do a flavor of the day."

"Nice touch." Blake poured himself a cup, giving it a sniff. "It smells nice. Too bad we ate all the pastries."

"We'll have about a thousand of them to eat next week," Sarah teased, earning a laugh from the others.

Blake slurped noisily, then chided, "Hey, I'm not the only taster. Everyone grab a cup. Be sure you try them all." Turning to face them, he caught the dull expression in his enforcer's eyes. Making his way through as the girls crowded in, he clapped his friend on the shoulder. "Hang in there, buddy. She loves you, and I think eventually she'll come around."

Rider winced. "Is it that obvious?"

"Yeah." Blake grinned behind his paper container, cutting him a sideways glance. "The dark circles give it away. But don't worry, she just hides hers with coverup."

Rider snorted a short laugh, the grin lingering. "Thanks. I'd hate to think I was in misery alone." Glancing around to be sure their conversation was private, he added, "In more serious news, what have you decided to do about our little miscreant? Should we drag him in for questioning? Try out the new toys?"

"Not yet." Blake gave his head a single shake. "But you know what they say. Keep your enemies close. He'll let his guard down if we just give him some room."

"Will do, boss," Rider agreed.

Once everyone had been served, and the comparisons completed, Blake held up his hand. "Listen up, everyone. I know this has been fun, but it's time to call it for the evening. We only have a few more days to clean and get everything set up before the grand reopening."

Sarah giggled loudly, drawing a dark glance. "You have this all planned out, don't you, babe," she teased.

"As a matter of fact, I do. I never paid much attention to this place until Morcant left, but now that I'm in charge, I like the way I run things," he replied confidently.

Raising his warm brew, Rider toasted, "Hear hear," which received a quick second from the others.

"Anyway," Blake pressed on. "I'd like to invite Hannah over to the house tonight for dinner. I believe she has earned a seat at our table."

"Oh, I can't," she replied swiftly. "I have a date with snuggle bunny."

"Snuggle bunny?" Joseline quipped, making an odd expression at her brother's nickname.

"Bring him along," Blake said quietly. Every face pivoted to stare at him in unison. "What? Have I ever said I didn't like him?"

The group hemmed and hawed, discussing it for a moment before he held up his hand again. "All right, all right, all right!" his words tumbled out. "I'm going to make the effort to get to know him, ok? Shoot me later."

Hannah laughed. "Is it really ok if he comes?"

"I wouldn't have offered if it wasn't." Blake frowned. "But decide quick, before I change my mind."

"Then we'll be there," she promised with a wide grin.

"Excellent," he agreed, giving the air a fist pump. "Now let's get out of here."

TWO

Inside and Out

SITTING in Blake's kitchen hours later, the group enjoyed a hearty meal. Stabbing a bite of steak with his fork, Rider observed, "I'm beginning to wonder if there's anything else this group knows how to cook."

"Oh, you'll find out when fall ends and the patio is covered in snow," Blake countered.

"You don't cook on the grill in the winter?" Meri asked thoughtfully.

"Are you kidding? It will be below freezing for nearly three solid months," Sarah informed her incredulously. "Karen and I are from Atlanta," she added "The snow here is to the point of unbearable."

"Yes, I hate winter. I can't believe we're still here," Karen said with a laugh.

"Hey," Joseline whined. "I'll keep you warm, baby."

"Aww, thank you, love." The pair shared a kiss while everyone else did their best not to stare.

"If that doesn't answer your question, then no. There will be no grilled steaks this winter," Blake finished with a flourish of his silverware. "Homemade pizzas and spaghetti will rule."

"Well, I guess we could try some to that famous clam chowder," Merideth suggested.

"Now that is an idea," Rider seconded, giving her a nod.

Continuing to eat without reply, Meri's snub was picked up by all, bringing the mood down a notch as they finished the meal. As soon as everyone was done, however, the dishes were quickly stacked, and the group moved to the living room, taking chairs from the kitchen to seat their growing numbers.

"I'm going out for a smoke." Blake swiped his box and lighter off the end table. "No one gets my seat!" he called back at them as he sauntered to the door.

"I'll go with you," Rider growled, cutting Meri an angry glare, then allowing the screen to slam as they exited.

"You're never going to get back in her pants that way," Blake reminded him once they were outside. Holding a smoke between his lips, he applied the flame to ignite it.

"I don't care. I'm getting very tired of being nice to her only to be ignored. Or worse," Rider grumbled.

"Well then, stop being nice. You're too obvious at it anyways. But that doesn't mean you have to be hateful." Blake took a long drag, then sent the smoke billowing from his lips. "Just be…ambivalent."

"Ambivalent? That'll win her over," Rider scoffed. His features twisted into a small pout, he took a seat on the steps and picked at a patch of tall grass.

"Whatever, man." Blake shook his head. What was the good of sound advice if his friend never listened?

When they went back inside a few minutes later, Hubert paused in the middle of his story. Blinking up at Blake, he waited.

"Go on. Don't quit on my account," the owner of the house insisted, sliding into his favorite cushioned chair.

Bert shrugged, not accustomed to friendly banter with the coven's magister. "Sorry, I forgot where I was."

Grinning, Joseline led with a reminder, and Blake stared at him until the tale was complete. "That was pretty funny," he observed, cutting the woman a quick wink.

"Hey, did anyone notice that the shopping center across from the store sold?" Karen pointed out excitedly. "I guess we're going to get new neighbors soon. Maybe it will give us even more traffic."

"Yes, it was a shame all three businesses went under during the pandemic," Sarah lamented. "I wonder who will be moving in."

Blake appeared uncomfortable with the conversation. "What makes you think anyone will?" he asked, shifting in his seat.

"Well, the realtor sign was gone this morning," Merideth pointed out. "One can only assume."

"Been watching the place, have you?" Rider clipped.

"It's a prime piece of storefront," she snapped. "If we ever wanted to expand, or anything..." her voice trailed away at his scrutiny. "I don't have to explain myself to you," she finished hotly.

Getting to his feet, Blake pulled a wad of keys out of his pocket. "I was saving this, but since you noticed the sign, I might as well tell you. But we still have a grand reopening next week, so don't everyone scatter at once."

Looking at the bundle, he pulled out a small ring with a few shiny pieces of metal on it. "Joseline, this set is for you. It goes to the smaller building on the west end. It has some floor space, in case you want to open your storefront again in a better location, but mostly I figure you will move your equipment over so you can continue your production and be closer to the rest of us."

Rising slowly, she gaped at him. Accepting the ring, she stared at it. "You're giving me a new location?" She looked up, her eyes meeting his. "You bought that building!"

Blake cocked his head to the side, giving her a sly grin, then pumped his eyebrows at her. "I bought that building." Fishing out another set, he transitioned smoothly. "Rider, you get the main retail space in the center."

"Holy shit." Rider got to his feet, standing before him. "I don't have enough work to fill that kind of square footage!" He swallowed, the keys heavy in his hand. "I never realized how many hours of work were in the gallery until it went up in flames."

"Take your time. You do fabulous work, brother. The studio will be there to display it when you're ready."

Rider stepped forward, catching the other man off guard with a hug. Slapping him on the back, he muttered, "Thanks, man. I really appreciate this."

"You're welcome." Blake gave him a firm rub before pushing him away. "Now, for the final set." He pivoted, facing Merideth, who sat at his feet in a straight-backed chair. "I know that selling coffee and trinkets is fun for a while, but it's not really what either of you girls have your hearts set on. You also deserve a place to call your own, where your dreams can soar."

Meri and Hannah exchanged a glance. "Does he mean us?" Hannah mouthed, to which Merideth only nodded with a shrug.

"Of course I mean you." Blake laughed heartily, giving the set a jingle. "You two get the east end, which has no real sales floor. It's more of an office, since you both really work at the homes of your clients. And since there's only one space left, the two of you will have to share."

"But we do different things," Meri clarified, standing slowly beside him.

"Yeah, sort of." Blake bobbled his head. "You actually do the same thing. Inside and out." He grinned at her.

"Inside and out," Hannah repeated, also rising as her excitement grew. "Shut the front door, what a cute name!"

Meri exposed her palms, silently asking her friend to explain.

"Inside and Out Home Décor!" Hannah nearly shouted. "You do the inside, and I design the patios and yards!"

"Oh my gosh!" Merideth squealed as the light came on. Hopping in a small circle together, the two girls caught each other in a firm hug.

"So, do I have a place in this little scenario?" Hubert asked quietly. "Or am I the dope stuck at the old location."

"No, silly!" Joseline pulled him to his feet. "You're my partner, thick and thin. But we can certainly turn the old location into storage. The temperature control is perfect, and we can get ahead for the good times when we are selling over what we can produce."

"Yeah, that makes sense," he agreed, not really sure she wanted him there.

Leaving the group, Blake had almost made it to the stairs before Sarah caught him. "Where are you going, Mister?"

"Oh, just giving them a few minutes to celebrate." Sliding in behind her as she faced the crowd, he wrapped his arms around her growing belly. Laying his hands on her bump, they watched the others chatter. "You think they like them?"

"Oh, gosh! They love it! You are such a kind and generous man." She grinned, patting him gently. "Which reminds me, we need to talk about the wedding. I've gotten started on my plans, but I'm really afraid to get too far in... until we've talked to my parents."

"Then book us a flight. We can miss a few days," he advised, giving her a squeeze before dropping his hold and continuing up to their room.

THREE

Homeward Bound

"I LIKE THESE COLORS, but the material is kind of icky feeling," Sarah pointed out to her friends, fingering the selection spread on the large breakroom table of the shop.

Meri looked over the swatches she and Hannah had gathered. "Well, they are mostly for color reference."

"Yeah. We can go with a different material if these don't suit," the blonde agreed.

"Ok, let's go with this seafoam green for the dress. I really like that." Sarah held up the strip next to her hair. "It goes well, don't you think?"

"Are you sure you don't want a white gown?" Karen asked, wrinkling her nose.

"Tradition says I shouldn't," Sarah informed her with a sigh.

"A very outdated tradition," Merideth pointed out, rolling her eyes.

"Hey, are you girls going to be much longer?" Joseline asked, joining them from upstairs. "The guys are doing their best up there, but Rider isn't much a floor hand."

"Only a few more minutes." Sarah began gathering the

bits of cloth. "I think we have what we need. I never imagined how much work went into a business."

"Yes, and soon we will be down one," Meri pointed out, eyeing her friend's growing bulge.

"Not until next year," Sarah corrected, her hand automatically drawn to the bump. "And I think Blake is going to hire more help. He said we needed a proper schedule, rather than all hands on deck as we have been. He wants to be sure we are all getting days off effective immediately."

Karen nodded, thinking of the time she could spend doing other things. "It would be nice not to feel guilty when I'm away."

"Are you sure she can make the dress and it will fit in a few weeks?" Sarah asked, presenting Hannah with the correct color selection.

"Yes. I'll tell her you want the silky cloth underneath and the lacy covering you picked out. She is going to dye it, so it will be the color you want. And it is going to be light and airy, so there will be plenty of room even if you are a bit larger than your measurements. It's a daytime wedding, right?"

"Yeah, Halloween is my birthday, so I'm used to doing all the private stuff early so everyone can still do their night thing. Otherwise, no one shows up."

Karen dropped her arm over her friend's shoulder. "You are never going to forget that one party, are you."

"No one came." Sarah shrugged. "I didn't think it was a big deal to give up trick-or-treating but apparently it was." She smiled at her friend, who had always been there for her. "You're ok with the darker green for the Maid of Honor dress, right?"

"Of course! It's your special day, and I will wear a tow sack if you want me to."

Contents

The group laughed as they made their way out the door. "I certainly hope it doesn't come to that." Sarah sighed. "I thought this was going to be a small, simple wedding, but it seems to get more complicated every day."

Fortunately for her, each friend had agreed to handle one portion of the planning. Hannah was securing the dress, and she had that well in hand. Merideth had arranged for chairs, an arch, and decorations, and was giving it her best to keep it small for her dear friend. Joseline, of course, was dipping special candles and calling in a florist that she knew, who would have the arrangements all ready for the big day. And finally, Karen had contracted a delectable selection of foods and beverages for a buffet style reception, with a beautifully simple wedding cake.

"Don't worry," Meri soothed as they reached the top of the incline. "We are each doing our part. All you have to do is help with the selections, and this is going to be a fabulous wedding."

Scattering when they hit the floor, the girls took over, allowing the men of their coven to retreat to the rooms below. Pulling out a fresh tome, Rider open it on the vacated table and slipped into his chair. Blake waved to his enforcer after filling his mug, ready to tackle the deposit and sales reports.

"Hey, Blake," Rider called after him. "Yeah?" The other man paused in the doorway, taking a noisy sip. "What's up?"

"I'm not sure I gave you proper thanks for the gallery space," Rider offered, fidgeting with his pen, his note page ready to go. "I've been thinking about it, and I'm not sure I can pull it off alone."

"Well, I bought the building. You can consider me your partner, if you like," Blake offered. "I thought you ran the studio in NOLA."

"I did, but I had help. Robert provided at least as much

artwork as I did. And there, I felt…inspired. The area spoke to me. I know that I belong here, but it isn't home." Rider hung his head. "I guess what I mean is, I haven't found what moves me about this place yet."

"There's no rush, my friend. We own that building outright, so we're not losing anything. If it sits empty while you figure it out, I'm ok with that." Blake inhaled deeply. "I know what it's like to feel lost. Don't let it get you down. It will click when it clicks." Looking around at the paintings Merideth had chosen, he added, "You should get out more. Take some walks. Hell, take a few days and go visit some places. You never know when that lightening is going to strike."

"Thanks, man." Rider looked up at him and grinned. "I don't want to get too far away though. You never know when you're going to need some enforcing." He chuckled, indicating the chamber behind him with a stiff thumb.

"Well, we can always hope that room collects dust, and we never have to use it." Blake slapped the door frame before he left, ready to get on his pile of paperwork, and hoping his friend would find his way home.

FOUR

Not to Coven

THE FOUR FRIENDS left for Atlanta three weeks before Halloween. They weren't sure how Sarah's parents were going to react, but she had called ahead to let them know that they were coming.

"Calm down," Joseline whispered in Karen's ear as they stood waiting to board their flight.

"How can I?" Karen replied, grinning at her best friend. "I haven't seen my parents in *years*."

"Neither have I, but you don't see me bouncing around like a wild woman," Sarah observed. She might have been giddy as well, but having been transformed into Brenna two years before had complicated things, and she wasn't looking forward to explaining it to anyone, let alone her parents.

"Let her be anxious if she wants to," Blake corrected. "You girls are taking a taxi, right?" He pointed to Jos and Karen in turn.

"Yes. My parents have moved to a suburb on the opposite side of the city, so we will have a bit of a drive to get there both ways. No time for a big get together, I'm afraid," Karen lamented.

"It's fine. We won't keep you at the airport, in case Sarah's father is late. Go catch a cab, have a pleasant holiday, and we'll see you back at the boarding gate going home on Thursday," Blake suggested.

"Wow. Two whole days with just us." Joseline's eyes twinkled. "How will we ever manage?"

"Just be careful," Blake warned. He looked Karen up and down. "If you feel the need to practice, do it discreetly. Now that you know your talent, you might be tempted, but no one must see it."

"I think I'll take a rest from practicing," she assured him, stepping up to give him a hug. Turning to Sarah, she did the same. "Be safe," she whispered in her ear.

"I have my shining knight," Sarah countered, patting the girl on the back. "I'll see you on Thursday."

Boarding the plane, their seats weren't together, so Sarah was glad they had said their goodbyes beforehand. "Down to the two of us," she breathed, sinking into her spot next to the window.

"Three," he corrected, glancing at her bump.

"Soon," she agreed. Sitting back to get comfortable, she rubbed her belly and thought of her dear friend. When they were airborne, she pushed the button to recline and pondered aloud. "I wonder why Meri hates to fly so much." Glancing out at the puffy clouds, she sighed. "I find it rather peaceful, being up here. It's like a mini holiday, away from the bustle of life."

"Our lives have been pretty busy as of late. Which is a nice change after all those months of being shut in," Blake observed. Glancing around them, the plane buzzed with people. "We should catch a nap," he suggested. "This trip may be busy as well."

Watching her sleep a few minutes later, he smiled to

himself, remembering how they met and the darkness that stalked her. It had worried him, coming there, and explaining her changed being to her parents. He might have tried to hide her alterations, but in the end decided they would face whatever music played. Besides, she would never have found peace if they hadn't. Daring to stroke her limp hand on the armrest between them, he whispered, "May you find what you need, my darling."

Once they were on the ground, Blake laughed as Karen and Joseline wasted no time exiting the plane and they were gone before he and Sarah ever made it out of the tunnel. "I see they took our advice to heart."

"Right. Why wait for the fat, pregnant girl." Sarah grinned, despite her harsh words.

Blake shook his head, recalling her chubby previous physique. "You aren't fat, love. You are a twig, which is why your belly shows so much."

"Har-har," she shot back. "I can live with it, I guess."

They each had a carry on, and had not checked any baggage, so they were able to exit to the loading and unloading lanes straight away. Rolling hers beside her, Sarah mumbled, "Dad said he still has his old F150 single cab."

"What color is it?"

"Dark blue."

"I see him." Blake pointed. "This may be awkward when we walk up. If he makes a scene, we calmly leave, you understand? We'll catch a taxi and find a hotel until Thursday."

"You think he won't like the new me?" She giggled anxiously. "Or is he going to be pissed that you knocked me up."

"He's going to be something," Blake said, strolling beside her. "Mr. Matthews," he called when they were close, offering his hand.

Taking the appendage, Tim shook it while looking the girl up and down.

"I know. I'm not what you expected." Sarah waited, unsure what to say next.

Her father stared at her, pursing his lips. "On purpose?" he asked.

Confused by the question, she blurted, "No, I didn't do this on purpose!" Then she cupped her belly and grinned. "Well, the baby is on purpose. The extreme makeover, definitely not." Turning to her mate, she added, "This is Blake Korrigan. My fiancé."

"Korrigan?" Tim gaped at him, wiping the hand he had used to shake with down the front of his plaid shirt.

"I guess you've heard of us." Blake squirmed. "Would you like to go somewhere and discuss things, or should we just get back on the plane?"

Tim looked between them doubtfully. "They're expecting us at the house. The little wife and some of Sarah's friends from school have made up a big welcome home dinner. It might be best if we didn't disappoint them."

Sarah grinned at her father's southern drawl. "It's good to be home, Daddy." Climbing into his truck, she wiggled into the middle of the bench seat.

Tossing their bags in the bed, Blake took the passenger side, sandwiching her between them. Once they were rolling, he observed, "You don't seem very surprised at Sarah's new look." Something didn't fit, and he needed to figure it out quick.

"We were warned when she was born it might happen," the driver explained curtly. "That mark on her leg was a curse, or so we were led to believe."

Blake grinned, exhaling a short sigh of relief. Meeting

Sarah's quizzical gaze, he nodded. "Your parents are familiar with the craft."

"Familiar, yes, but we set it aside when Sarah was a baby," Timothy explained, maneuvering the vehicle through traffic. "We've had no contact with the coven or anyone else associated for some time."

"But you recognize my name. Or that of my family, to be precise," Blake observed, watching him over the red hair between them.

"We used to know of a Korrigan, back in the day. Speaking of which, I need to warn her mother. Our party guests are in for a real surprise." Tim's round belly shook when he laughed.

"I don't see how that's funny." Sarah sniffled, holding her bump.

Wearing a scowl, Blake turned to the window, watching as the city disappeared behind them and the cars thinned out. "How far before we get there?" he asked curtly.

"Bout fifteen minutes." His call was answered, and Tim's voice boomed. "Honey. Honey? You got them tables and stuff all ready in the back yard?" He waited. "Yeah, I got her, but… yeah I know it was a surprise." He looked at the young woman next to him. "But she's not the girl she used to be, sweetheart. You need to meet us in the living room and have a look before you take her outside." He glanced at the device. "We lost the connection."

"Or she hung up." Blake turned to glare at him. "Don't worry about your guests. I'll make sure they see no difference."

"How are you going to do that?" Sarah asked quietly, more confused with every mile the truck traveled.

"Just relax, sweet pea. I know a way." He lay his arm across her shoulders, drawing her against him. When they pulled up in front of a simple, white, two-story house, he climbed out, helping her to exit the vehicle. Leaning in, he whispered, "Stay close to me."

Taking the path to the front door, the trio went inside, where Tanya impatiently waited. "Where's Sarah?" she asked, looking past them at the screen.

"This here is Sarah," Tim stated firmly, waiting for her to catch up.

"Oh my God." The woman grasped her by the arms, pulling at her this way and that as she inspected her. Dropping her hold, she scolded her husband. "You told them, didn't you."

"Not much." He shrugged. "But obviously, the curse has come true."

"You knew about my curse?" Sarah flicked her gaze between them. They had never breathed a word about it to her.

"Well, honey, you did have that strange birthmark when you were born," her mother pointed out. "We were told it was the mark of a curse. So, we took you away in hopes it would never be brought into being. For all the good it did us." The woman fidgeted, still inspecting her daughter. "And why are you pregnant?"

"I guess she failed to mention that when she called," Blake pointed out, crossing his arms. "Are there people outside waiting?"

"Yes, as a matter of fact there are," Tanya recalled, glancing over her shoulder at the door that exited the kitchen. "What are we going to do?"

"I need a picture of her, as she was," the magister instructed. "I'll take care of the rest."

"You can use the one on the wall," Sarah suggested, pointing to her high school graduation photo.

Lifting it from the nail, Blake nodded. "This will do nicely."

"Well, give me a minute. I need to go pee," Sarah called, starting up the stairs. "This kid has been sitting on my bladder the whole way here."

Blake frowned as she disappeared. He pivoted, looking around the house while they waited. When his eyes reached them, the couple standing side by side staring at him felt out of place. "You are not her parents," he stated curtly.

Her jaw dropped, but Tim held up his hand to keep his wife silent. "What makes you think that?"

"I don't know. This whole place seems…odd. You seem odd." He indicated the pair, wafting the picture at them. "You don't even seem that happy to see her."

Tanya shrugged. "She doesn't know. And from the looks of things, we have failed in our mission, so why pretend?"

Hearing her footsteps above them, Blake sighed. "Care to tell me about your mission? Or is it a secret?" he hissed, not understanding how anyone could show such indifference to a child that they had raised. Surely they had to feel something at seeing her again.

Scowling, Tim crossed his arms over his chest, resting it on his large, pot belly. "We left the coven to protect her. They said she was cursed, as it was told in widow Korrigan's journal."

"So, you do know my family," Blake surmised.

"Only the widow. She's an old crone, but she disappeared for long times. Then she'd turn up. Crazy woman," Tanya explained.

"And she told you to hide Sarah," Blake presumed.

"No. She told her parents to, but they weren't having it." Tim pointed a finger at him. "So, we took her and left the coven. If this curse couldn't find her, it couldn't come to fruition."

"But we failed," Tanya lamented, glancing again at the back of the house. "We should send them home. Tell them to forget it. Her plane crashed or something."

Blake shook his head, then pinched the bridge of his nose, unable to fathom that these simpletons had raised his beloved. "I'll take care of Sarah. She will enjoy the party. And when we leave here Thursday morning, she will never return. The two of you can go back to whatever life you enjoyed before. Until then, please do your best to be loving, doting parents, as I am sure you have always been."

The couple exchanged a glance, then Tanya raised her hands. "All right. I'll go start serving drinks and you can bring Sarah out when you're ready."

Descending into the room as her mother let the back door slam, Sarah jumped. "Sorry. I had to visit my old room. I don't think they have touched a thing!" She smiled at Blake, placing herself in front of him. "Where's Mom?"

"Serving drinks. And if you ask me, she already had a few," he observed, holding the picture up for a better view.

Watching him, Tim asked, "What are you going to do?"

"I'm going to give her a shimmer. Or glimmer as it is sometimes called," he explained.

"Oh my gosh, I saw that in one of your spell books!" As a master caster, she should have thought of that. "Blake, you're a genius!"

"I find that debatable, love. However, I do know a thing or two about hiding," he replied. Placing his hands on her shoulders, he instructed, "Stand up straight and close your eyes. That's it. Lean your head back just a little. Perfect." Wiping his lips, he glanced at Tim. "Don't worry. Only a powerful witch will be able to see through it. Everyone else will see her as they remember her. For a few hours at least."

He dropped the picture onto the back of the sofa next to him, then placed a hand on each side of her face.

"Have you done this before?" Tim's curiosity got the better of him as he leaned in for a closer look.

"A few times. A good witch only uses the magic that they must," Blake explained, as his thumbs gently caressed her closed lids. Bending forward, he kissed her forehead. "You are free to go," he whispered.

Blinking rapidly, Sarah looked about her. "I don't feel any different."

"She don't look any different, neither," Tim observed.

"That's because you know what she looks like," Blake explained. "Your wife will probably see her that way as well. Everyone else will be fooled."

"How long will it last?" Sarah asked, ready to try it out.

"A few hours. When you get up in the morning you will be yourself to all again." Blake indicated the door. "Shall we?" Following her into the bright sunlight, he allowed her to mingle. Always on her heels, he accepted hugs and handshakes when they were offered. His eyes never rested, and his mind remained alert until they finally turned in for the night, hours later.

"What a lovely day," Sarah breathed, stretching out on top of the comforter. "Did you like meeting my old friends?" she asked through a yawn.

"Yes, it was quite pleasant," he agreed. "I'm going down for a smoke. Do you need anything?" When she didn't respond, he turned, finding she had already drifted off to sleep.

Looking around, he pondered leaving her there alone. But he didn't want to smoke in her parents' house. Besides that, he needed to make a call. Taking his phone, he made it to the first floor. In the living area, her father sat reclined in front of a flickering television. "Where's Tanya?" he asked.

"She's done gone to bed. I'm headed that way myself," Tim drawled. Kicking the foot portion, he convinced it to lock and got to his feet. "Tanya and I've talked. You don't need to take her away from us. You go on home on Thursday, and we'll take care of her."

"But Sarah and I are getting married," Blake stammered, completely confused.

"Oh, that's right." Tim climbed onto the first step of the stairs. "In that case, I guess we'll need to be at the wedding. She'll want me to give her away and all."

Blake blinked at him, considering if he might have had too many of Tanya's cocktails. "I know of no such plan, but you are welcome to join us for the reception," he offered. As he took a few more steps, Blake considered following him. "You said you two were in a coven, right?"

"Yeah, we's based out of Savannah." Tim stopped at the landing and rubbed his round belly. "I don't know if they's still there."

"So, you grew up here in Georgia?"

"Yeah. Tanya and me's born and bred. But I'll have to get in the bed. We'll talk more about all that in the morning, Blake." Ending the conversation, Tim turned and completed the final section.

Standing on the floor, Blake could see the door to Sarah's room. Tim walked right past it, proceeding down the hall. Following up to the first landing he looked and listened, but saw nor heard any sign of him, or the sleeping Tanya. "These people are crazy," he muttered, returning to the living room. His mind made up, he exited through the kitchen door. Sitting on the narrow porch, he lit a smoke, then swiped his phone to make that call.

FIVE

Home Fires

"I CAN'T BELIEVE I'm going to meet your parents," Joseline squealed, squirming in the seat as they rode out of the city. "I haven't even taken you to meet mine."

"You will when you are ready," Karen clipped, reaching for her hand.

"Are you ready?" Joseline asked, turning to stare at her. "Or is this trip just convenient?"

Their eyes locked, Karen swallowed. "We're kismet, remember?"

"You say that often, love, but do you believe it in your heart of hearts?" Josee returned her gaze to the window. "I can't believe how warm it is here. The air is already chilly in Boston."

"We don't really have winter down here," Karen explained. "Not like we do back home."

Joseline gave her hand a squeeze, the words *back home* resonating within her. "I think we're ready," she whispered to herself. She knew it in her heart of hearts. "I can't wait," she said more loudly. "Do you know if they have been hiding their secret powers from you all these years?"

"I don't know," Karen replied, cutting her a sly grin. "I fear they are average ordinary mortals and I have no witch blood at all."

"Would that be so bad?" Joseline asked, her eyes wandering over her lover's slender form.

"Blake is something like a hundred and twenty years old," Karen explained quietly, watching the driver from behind. "He says that pureblood witches can live for centuries, and his blood is very pure. Is yours?"

"Oh, gosh, I guess that it is!" Joseline grinned excitedly. "I will age slowly and appear as young as he does for decades."

"I fear that I won't," Karen confessed glumly. Leaning her elbow against the window, she pressed her palm to her face. "I'll age like an old hag, and you will long to be rid of me."

Joseline gaped at her. "I never considered the possibility."

"Would it change your feelings for me?" Karen blinked back tears, her focus on the passing cars to keep them hidden.

"Never, my darling! We are kismet." Pulling at her, Joseline turn herself, sliding into the other girl's lap before pushing her to lie down in the seat. Straddling her, she giggled. "I'll make love to you right now, if you require a demonstration."

Casually, like a practiced old pervert, the driver grabbed the rearview mirror, giving it an adjustment. Catching the motion, Jos leaned in to whisper, "He wants to watch."

"Men always want to watch lesbians. And I'll take the demonstration tonight." Catching Josee's neck, she guided her down, kissing her deeply.

"I don't know if I can wait that long," Jos breathed. "Did you bring any toys?"

"What did you think I checked a bag for?" Karen giggled beneath her.

"Oh. I guess you didn't want to risk a scene at security?"

"Nope." Karen kissed her again, mingling their tongues as her groin tingled.

Sitting up, Joseline pulled Karen's thin frame up beside her, holding her in her arms. "We will enjoy the time we have, precious. If we are destined to be parted sooner rather than later, we will make love all of those days and be happy that we ever loved at all."

"Such a poet." Karen snickered. "You make it sound so beautiful."

"It is beautiful!" Twisting to see her better, Joseline smiled. "I feel it with all of my being. The poetry of our souls. Call me silly if you want to, but that is exactly how it should be. Love for the time we have and not waste a minute of it."

Turning into a new subdivision, Karen gasped. "I think we're here!"

"A few more blocks," the driver agreed. Glancing at the meter, he added, "This was an expensive ride."

Joseline pulled a hundred out of her purse, prepared to hand it to him. "We knew it would be. But worth it. We have to go back on Thursday. Would you be interested in the return trip?"

"Give me the time and I'll add it to my book," he agreed.

"You're a good man. This should cover it, and the rest is for you." Jos explained, handing him the money.

Setting their bags out of the trunk a few minutes later, the cabbie gave them a nod as he handed Joseline a card. "In case you need me before then, give a ring. I'll come or get you someone who is close by."

"Sounds wonderful," she cooed, accepting the number.

"Appreciate it, ladies. I'll see you on Thursday." He climbed behind the wheel and drove away.

"You just gave him a fifty-dollar tip," Karen observed.

"And we will get excellent service on Thursday, my dear." Hoisting her bag, she also took Karen's carry on. "Can you get the big one?"

"Girls!" A woman squealed, dashing out of the house to greet them. Her arms wide, she caught Karen first, hugging her tightly. Then turning to Joseline, she delivered the same. "I'm so glad to finally meet you!"

Joseline smiled sweetly. She had known Karen spoke of her to the parents, but how deeply the understanding went remained to be seen. Seeing a man also exit the structure, she waved. "I've got the little bags. Would you mind taking the large one? Karen's limp is a little strong today."

"It's from all that sitting," their daughter explained, holding her mother's hand as they strolled to the house and favoring her bum foot.

"I sure can," her jolly father agreed. "I just need to check the pit in a bit. The brisket will be done soon."

Inside, the three women agreed to meet in the kitchen after the girls had settled into the guest room. "What do your parents know about me?" Joseline asked when they got there.

"I've told them we are a couple. I think they understand," Karen informed her with a nod.

"But are we hiding our powers from them? Or should we hint and fish a bit?"

"I think we should hide." Grasping her hands, Karen shook her head. "Honestly, I have seen no sign that they would have the foggiest about the craft."

"Then I will wear my normal hat as long as I can," Joseline agreed. Leading her out, they found the kitchen. "Carol, your house is divine! Is it only the two bedrooms?"

"Thank you! And yes, opposite sides of the house. Wonderful for privacy." She stirred a large salad as she continued. "We bought it a few years ago, after Karen left for college. This is our retirement dream." The older woman beamed, and Joseline could sense the joy within her, but little else.

Eating, talking, and whiling away the hours, Karen's prediction appeared to be true, and by the time the couple retired for the evening, they both were convinced they were average ordinary mortals.

"So where do I get my gift from, I wonder?" Karen asked, once they were in their room and door had been closed and locked, just to be safe. Tempted, she used her powers to peel back the blankets and expose the sheets. "I am getting better at it."

"All things with practice," Joseline agreed. "Madame Demore is a mortal. Sometimes it just crops up."

"I'm afraid that's not where it came from, though." Karen sighed, sitting on the edge of the bed she had unmade. "What if it's some kind of transfer from Morcant? Or his mother? Maybe they gave me a bum foot *and* the use of the craft."

"Who knows." Joseline flopped open the larger suitcase and gasped. "You didn't bring one, you brought a dozen!" Lifting a large floppy one, she giggled. "I'm going to use it on you."

"No, I don't really like that one," Karen whined.

"Then why did you bring it?"

"I had the room?" Karen shrugged. "Seriously. My leg is tired. I'll just do you and we can call it a night."

"You're scared your parent's will hear us," Joseline teased, the tip of her tongue licking the toy. "She said the house was designed for privacy, remember?"

"Well, it's my parent's house. I've never had sex under their roof. Can't we just wait. Maybe tomorrow I'll be ready."

"Not a chance." Jos dropped the dildo on the blanket next to her, urging her to the center of the plush surface. "Let me give you a little fat Freddy action."

"Oh God." Peals of laughter escaped Karen's glistening lips. "I love how you name them, but why are they always guys?"

"Because. They're dicks." Joseline grinned at her.

Giggling loudly at the pun, Karen tensed when Joseline's hand caught her hair and nudged it out of the way. The straps on her tank top not completely covering her bra, Jos was able to snag both and slide them off a smooth, tan shoulder in a single movement. The backs of her fingers trailing down a supple arm, Karen groaned.

Joseline leaned over her, nuzzling her ear to whisper, "I'm going to fuck you raw. Me and fat Freddy."

Karen shivered beneath her. With nimble fingers, she caught the hem of Josee's shirt. Lifting it, she slid her thumb under the edge of the lace covering and removed it from her breast. Sliding up, Joseline offered the pink nipple for tasting. Karen's tongue made a single lap around it before she pulled the toy away.

Slithering down her body, Joseline kissed and bit as she went, removing the thin shirt and the bra beneath it. At the pants, she unbuttoned and unzipped, then tugged them down her legs.

Raising her rear, Karen assisted in the process. Glancing at fat Freddy, her pulse quickened. The coverings removed from her legs, Joseline fondled her clit, then licked at it. Grasping the jelly dildo, she used it to massage the folds of flesh before giving her just enough of it to make her squirm.

An ache formed deep inside her, and Karen sobbed, "You're torturing me."

"Say his name. Tell me you want it," Joseline commanded, lightly pinching her labia with her teeth.

"Fat Freddy," Karen groaned, spreading her legs wider. "Give it to me, baby."

Pushing it in, Jos rolled it around, stretching and filling Karen's pussy. When it stopped sliding easily, she withdrew about an inch, then pumped it there.

Lifting her hips against it, Karen gasped for air. "Shit. I'm gonna cum. In my momma's house," she wheezed. Raising her knees, her feet on the mattress, she thrust against the toy, Joseline's fingers brushing her lips where she held it. "Oh, your hand," she groaned.

Holding Freddy in, Joseline added a twisting motion so that her fingers ground against her lover's flesh. "Raw, baby," she growled.

Clinging to the blankets, the cascade fell without warning, Karen chirping and grunting loudly. Afraid the noise might be heard, privacy or not, Joseline clamped her free hand over her mouth, only partially muffling the sound.

As the last quiver pulsed through Karen's body, her phone rang, somewhere beneath them.

SIX

What Happens in Georgia

"SHIT, WHERE IS IT?" Karen gasped. Tearing Freddy out of her cunt, she rolled over and searched for the device.

"Found it," Joseline called, locating it under the edge of the bed.

"Fuck, it's Blake." Inhaling deeply, Karen paused, then accepted the call with a calm, "Hello?"

"Karen, it's Blake."

"Yeah, I know who it is," she growled. "I also know what time it is. Aren't you guys busy having sex or something at this hour?"

"Naw, Sarah's asleep," he admitted. "She's gone from the tired from hormones phase to the exhausted from carrying around a baby phase, I think."

"Great. What do you want?" Karen glanced at Joseline, who sat next to her, patiently listening.

"I need to see what you can tell me about Sarah's parents," he gushed.

"You called me. After midnight. To ask me. About her mom and dad?" Jos had gone down on her and licked at her juicy wetness.

"Yes. Something is wrong here. Her parents aren't really her parents, Karen."

Something in his voice demanded Karen's attention. Pushing against Joseline's head, she closed her legs. "What the hell is that supposed to mean? Wouldn't she know if they weren't her parents?"

"I mean, they've never been her parents. They recognized my family name. Korrigan. After that, they started acting all kinds of weird. I really think we need to get out of here," he finished in a rush.

Able to hear Blake's voice from her position, Joseline sat up stiffly. Pulling her own cell out of her purse, she located the cabbie's card. "Earl," she read to herself. Typing in the number, she asked, "What's the address?"

Karen rolled it off to her from memory. At Joseline's surprised expression, she shrugged. "I used to live on the same street."

"What's going on?" Blake demanded. "Hello! Are you still there?"

"I'm here." Karen giggled. "I think Jos is sending a cab for you."

"A cab? At this hour?"

"He gave us his card. She tipped him pretty good, so he might do it," Karen explained.

"He can't get there until after five. Maybe five-thirty," Joseline informed her.

"Can you be out front of the house at five-thirty?" Karen asked.

"Yeah. We can do that. I just want to get away from here without either of them knowing."

"Great, we'll see you in the morning." Karen ended the call. "Of all the rotten timing," she muttered, gapping her legs to examine her swollen vulva. "Fuck."

"Did it hurt when you rolled over?" Joseline asked, examining the area. "I didn't think about that."

"It wasn't real comfortable," Karen admitted. "I freaked about the phone and just ripped it out of me."

"I'm sorry." Joseline appeared remorseful. "No more fat Freddy for you."

"That's ok, I'm going to wash him and use him on you!" Karen announced, leaping off the bed and a carrying it into the bathroom.

"Shouldn't we get some sleep? I mean if Blake and Sarah are coming here in a few hours?" Joseline suggested.

"It will take them at least an hour to get here, if the traffic is good, and two if it's even moderately bad. I think we have time to get you a quickie," Karen purred as she returned and rolled the other girl onto her back.

"Sarah?" Blake shook her gently. "Come on, baby, it's time to go."

"Go where?" Sarah said loudly before he hushed her.

"We need to be quiet. I want to leave and not have your parents know we've gone," he confessed.

"What? Why?" She sat up, looking around the dimly lit room. "Is that a candle?"

"Yes. It gives us enough light to move around, but not much as far as alerting the world that we are," he explained. Holding up a loose leg, he helped her put on a pair of her stretchy pants.

"But why are we running away? I thought I got two days."

"Well, that's hard to explain. It's been bothering me since we got here, and it's one of those mysteries I'd rather not solve face to face with them," he offered. "Karen is sending a cab for us, and we are going to go crash with her parents for a day, then we go home."

Digging in her bag, he produced socks. Getting them on her feet, he added the shoes. "I don't dress other people very often," he observed. "Am I doing it right?"

"It feels fine." She yawned wide. "What time is it?"

"The taxi will be out front at five-thirty. We have about ten minutes to clear out of here and creep downstairs…nice and quiet."

"Ok, if you think that we should. I have to admit, it felt a little odd coming home."

Blake paused, looking up at her. "Why do you say that?"

"Well, when I called, they seemed pretty excited, but when I got here, they weren't very huggy or any of that," she pointed out. "It was kind of bleh."

"I'm sorry sweety. I have so many questions right now," he supplied, shoving things back in their bags.

"Do you think they are other people using the glimmer?" she asked, stopping his movements cold.

Pivoting, he stared at her, having had the same thought. "But who would know we were coming here? And why would they do that?" Besides, he would expect he could see through such a spell. That's why he didn't bother trying to fool them with it before they got there. His heart racing, he zipped the bag. "Forget the rest. Let's get out of here." Standing, he blew out the candle and stood next to the exit.

Opening the door, Blake peered into the dark hallway. Not a sound could be heard in the blackness. Adjusting the bags over his shoulder he held out his hand. When she didn't take it, he grabbed for hers.

"Bla—"

"Shh."

Pulling at her appendage, he guided her out into the hallway. Her room the last before the stairs, he looked back towards her parents' room. The door closed, he had no idea if they were on the other side, or even down below, waiting for them. It was a chance they had to take.

Moving a few steps, he reached the banister. Grasping it firmly with his free hand, he took a step down, then waited for her to brush against the back of them. Another step and another wait. The darkness thick and heavy, he couldn't imagine it being like that on any other night, as it had not been that dark when he came down before.

When they reached the bottom, light from outside shone in the windows of the kitchen, adding an eerie glow to the room. Pulling her behind him, he reached the front door. "God, I hope there's no alarm on this door," he muttered, twisting the locks, and freeing the latch.

Flinging the portal open, they hit the porch as lights skimmed across their bodies. Gently closing the heavy door behind them, Blake guided her down the few steps and out to the waiting cab.

Opening the back door, Black chunked their bags in, then guided her into the seat. Pushing her over enough to get himself in, he commanded, "Go" before he had even pulled it shut.

"Are you guys ok?" the man in the front seat drawled. "Your girlfriends were worried about you. Nice couple."

"Yeah, we're better now," Blake agreed, opening and re-shutting the door to close it properly. "In-laws."

Earl laughed. "I can relate. You might as well get comfortable. Your friends are on the other side of Atlanta."

"Just get us there in one piece," Blake requested, then

assured, "I'll definitely make it worth your while." Laying his arm across Sarah, he curled her against his chest. "Get some sleep, Baby. We have no idea what tomorrow will bring."

SEVEN

Pretty Lady

MERIDETH AWOKE EARLY. Lying in her double bed, she stared at the ceiling, mentally preparing herself for the day ahead. With four of their crew gone the day before, things at the store had been rough, and for the first time since he gave her the key to her new building, she seriously considered walking over and having a look.

Of course, Hannah had been over to look around twice. She had come back both times buzzing about it. But Meri hadn't been overly excited about anything in weeks, at least not for very long. Nothing sustained her. Not since Rider had basically ruined everything they had.

"This isn't getting me anywhere," she reminder herself sternly. Throwing off the covers, she rolled to the side of the bed and pushed her arms over her head, bending and flexing them. Standing, she did a few more stretches that helped get her moving. Turning to the wide mattress, she spread the sheet, then the blanket on top of it. Smoothing it, she fluffed the pillows and placed them perfectly between the sides.

In the kitchen, she added water to her tiny pot, scowling at the device. She had purchased it to avoid trips to the kitchen, where she might run into Rider, who was often showing his ass. She thought about the first day they were in Boston. Standing in Spellbound and looking for their sister, that's the way Blake had described him.

"It totally fits," she mumbled.

When the dripping ceased, Merideth emptied it into an oversized mug and took a short sip. Tilting her head back, she closed her eyes and enjoyed the feeling of that first taste clear to her soul.

In the connecting bathroom, she heard the water kick on for the shower. "Great. He beat me to it." They had worked together an entire day, and she had said less than ten words to him. "He's horrible at it." She sneered at his running, scattered around the store. "Good luck managing an art gallery," she tossed at the wall.

Setting her mug on the table, she flicked on the overhead lights. Making a pass through her small apartment, she ensured that everything was clean, every item in its place. Gathering her clothes, she folded them onto the foot of the bed. Retrieving the coffee, she took a few more sips, then marched over to the bathroom door to bang on it a savagely.

"I'd like a hot shower, too," she yelled through the crack.

"There's plenty," his muffled reply reached her.

"Asshole." Fidgeting, she looked around for something else to do, and the sound of water running ended. "About damn time," she said loud enough he might here, then dropped her voice to add, "I hope he gets dressed in his room."

Making another pass around the apartment, she adjusted a few things. Rinsing her empty mug in the small sink, she set it on its place along the back of the counter, then jumped when her bathroom door opened suddenly.

"It's all yours," Rider called to her, crossing to his side, and giving that one a slam.

"Thanks. I'm sure Mother will appreciate that." Ezamay had come back to stay at the mansion since the girls were in Atlanta, and her room was above his, meaning she heard every sound that went on, especially if it were loud.

Marching over to the cubical, Meri stepped in and closed the door. Locking the one on his side, she stripped and cut on the spray. Stepping under, she moaned at the pleasure the warm cascade provided. Lathering herself, she sang softly, her voice echoing in the small space. Then she worked a dab of shampoo into her hair, not quite ready to rinse it when the water began to chill.

"Shit!" she sputtered, shoving her head under the cold spray. "Mother fucker!" she added, the easy, warm sensation she had been nurturing gone. Her hair rinsed the best she could, she slapped the handle, cutting off the shower in disgust.

Grabbing her towel, Meri applied it vigorously to her skin and hair, then wrapped it around her at the chest, the width of it falling to barely cover her privates. Unlocking Rider's side, she pushed it open, ready to give him an earful.

Instead, she found herself standing in a very cluttered room, no Rider in sight. Pushing the damp hair out of her face, it dripped on her bare shoulders as her eyes swung the arc of his quarters. "What a mess," she grumbled.

The wardrobe stood open, with clothes on most of the hangers. The bottom held a small pile that flowed out onto the floor. She wrinkled her nose, considering if they were clean or dirty.

On the other side of the partial wall, the kitchenette had been converted into a painting studio, with pictures of varying degrees of completion lining the walls, the cabinet top, and even surrounding the small table. Only a trail provided room to walk through the entrance, to the sink, and to the bed, with its sheets and blanks twisted and piled upon it. "Ugh," she grunted, her eyes finishing the semi-circle to land on a familiar portrait. "Holy shit."

"What the hell are you doing in here?" Rider yelled from his entrance.

Flabbergasted, she looked like a fish out of water, opening and closing her mouth to gasp for air. On an easel, clean and pristine, almost as if it were the focal point of the room, sat the Pretty Lady. Positioned next to the bed, it gave her an odd feeling in the pit of her stomach.

"Snooping," she growled back, finally finding her voice. "You used all the hot water and I got hosed. I didn't even have my hair rinsed."

Shoving his hand in his pocket, Rider took a sip of the coffee he'd gone to fetch. "And that's my problem how?" He snickered, amused at the spectacle she made.

"You are incorrigible," she shouted, slamming the door as she left, forgetting all about her mother.

In the room above, Ezamay sighed. She liked being near to Merideth, especially with the girls away, but being this close to the feud between her and Rider put the older woman on edge. Deciding to get up and moving, she dressed in layers, as she could never quite stay comfortable throughout the day. Slipping on a pair of sneakers, she found her way downstairs. Discovering Rider's partial pot of coffee, she helped herself to a cup.

"The house sure is quiet with Blake and Sarah gone," she observed when Rider joined her.

"Sorry about the door," he replied. "I forget that you're here."

She studied him for a moment. "Twice?"

"Only once." He shrugged, taking a seat in one of the chairs. "Meri slammed it the second time."

Ezamay giggled, hiding her smile behind her cup, then taking a noisy sip. "Thank you for the coffee," she offered. "I can always tell when you made it."

"Because Merideth makes her own in her room?" he quipped.

"No. But that is a good point," she agreed. "No, I can tell because it's just the way I like it. And it's perfect every time."

"I doubt that," he replied, getting to his feet. Stomping through the living room, he pounded on Meri's door. "I'm leaving in five minutes. If you're not out here, you can take the bus."

"Don't you dare," Merideth squealed, opening the portal. "I may not be your girl anymore, but you could at least show me a little courtesy."

"Five minutes," he repeated, holding up his hand and extending the digits. "I want to get up there and make sure everything is ready when it's time to open."

Meri didn't have time to argue. Throwing her makeup in a bag, she grabbed her brush and hair dryer. Adding a different blouse and a change of shoes, she stormed after him. "Don't you leave me!"

"Mind if I come today?" Ezamay asked from the kitchen when Merideth hit the living room.

Stopping, her daughter pivoted to look at her. "Mother. I didn't realize you were awake."

Standing, the other woman placed her cup in the sink. "I said, would it be all right if I joined you today."

"Well, I guess it would," Meri stammered. "But we need to get our asses in the car if we are riding with a— err Rider."

Grinning to herself, May followed her out front, locking

the door behind them. "May?" Rider asked when she started down the steps.

"Can I get a ride?" she asked jovially.

"I guess." He shrugged. "Meri, you take the back."

"I planned on it," she said curtly. Staring at the bag in her hand, she whispered Blake's spell, shrinking it by half. Dropping it in the rear seat, she climbed in next to it.

Rider grinned, hiding it from her as he slid behind the wheel. "You've become pretty resourceful," he offered, like an olive branch.

"And you've turned into a slob." She slapped it away.

"Oh no. I've always been casual with my place. When I don't have some fussy female living in it."

May sighed at their quarreling. Leaning against the window, she and her companions rode the rest of the way in silence, and she longed for a time the couple could at least get along.

EIGHT

Old Friends

"OH. MY. GOD." Carol clapped her hands to the sides of her face the moment she saw Sarah the following morning. "What beautiful red hair!"

Sarah smiled at her, and Blake pointed out, "We're hoping the baby gets it," earning him a surprised glance from his soon to be betrothed.

"I love it," Carol sang happily. Bouncing around her kitchen, she gathered utensils and pans to make breakfast.

"I hope you don't mind us crashing here with you," Sarah added shyly. "I never expected my father to be so upset!"

"You poor dear," the matron soothed. "People can be such old fuddy-duddies. In this day and age, a woman doesn't need a man's permission to have sex. To get married. Or to have a baby whenever she wants!"

"Carol," Andrew Hiltzman interjected, taking his favorite seat at their table. "I'm sure these nice young people didn't sign up for the lecture." He grinned at the foursome lining his breakfast bar.

"Actually, we already got one." Blake coughed a laugh.

"That's why we left." Sipping his coffee, he nodded at Karen's father.

"So, you two are getting married?" Carol asked, placing eggs on plates.

"On Halloween," Joseline chimed in. "We're helping to plan the wedding," she added, pointing to herself and their daughter.

"Oh, that's lovely. Karen used to have an old friend that was born on Halloween," Carol recalled. "Do you know Sarah, Brenna?" She paused in front of her, waiting for a response.

"You know, Boston is such a big place. I bet I know ten Sarahs." She shrugged.

"No, I don't think she knows Sarah Matthews, Mom." Changing the subject, she asked, "Do we have any syrup for the hotcakes?"

"There's a new jug in the pantry." Her father pointed.

"Well, this Sarah was a real sweet girl. Smart, too," the older woman pushed on. "Her parents were never too bright, though. I always found them a little odd."

Blake perked up at the mention of their previous hosts. "Well, that would be odd, wouldn't it? Parents typically have children that are fairly equivalent to themselves, wouldn't you think? At least in the intelligence department."

"Not in that family tree," Andy groused. "We lived down the street from them for twenty years, and I swear that man would forget which house was theirs." He looked around as the group laughed. "You think I'm joking, but before we moved, they got to taking in strange visitors, too. Almost like a bed and breakfast only for crazies."

"Maybe they were running a little Airbnb thing," Sarah suggested.

"That might be, but their house isn't really in the touristy part of the city. Anyone staying there would have to drive an hour or two to get anywhere worthwhile," he pointed out as Carol distributed hotcakes and sausage.

"Sounds like it might be a good thing we don't know this Sarah person," Blake said agreeably, adding salt and pepper to his eggs. "These little pancakes are delicious."

"So, what shall we do today, now that all your plans have been dashed?" Joseline asked between bites.

"Actually, Atlanta is a fine old city. I was thinking we might take a ride on one of the chain tours. If you're up to it, darling." Blake grinned at her encouragingly.

"That sounds wonderful," Sarah stammered. "Yes. And we'll get a hotel tonight, close to the airport. No sense bringing the cab back out here. We'd just be in the way."

Karen grinned. "Well, I'm glad you got to meet my Mom and Dad. And we'll see you at the airport for our flight home on Thursday."

"Sounds like a plan," Blake agreed cheerfully, offering his orange juice as a toast to the idea.

Inside a new taxi an hour later, Sarah leaned back against the seat and moaned. "This vacation is exhausting."

"Do you want to find a hotel now and make an early night of it?" Blake offered.

"What else did you have in mind? Surely we aren't really going on a tour." She had grown up there for fuck's sake. She could give the tour.

"No, that was just a cover." He chuckled at her relieved expression. "But I do have one place I'd like to visit, if you don't mind. We might be able to shed some light on exactly what is going on with your parents."

"If what they told you is true, they're not my parents," she denied sullenly. "But from the sounds of it, they are who they are supposed to be. Did you hear the way Mr. Hiltzman described them?"

"They were rather dim witted. She wanted to tell your friends your plane had crashed."

He snort-laughed, giving her a fit of giggles. Holding her belly, she let it roll for a moment before gathering herself under control. "Man, that felt good. We haven't laughed like that in a while."

"Maybe we should just take the day off. I'm sure there's some nice places to have a picknick or a good cup of coffee," he offered.

"I'd give anything for a glass of wine," she replied softly.

"Oh, honey."

"I know. And once the baby comes and then I finish nursing, I'll be able to drink again. Merideth was right. Having a baby is a huge sacrifice."

"You're going to nurse him?" Blake asked with wide eyes. "I thought everyone these days bought formula."

"Breast milk is better for the baby," she explained. "I want to give him or her every thing I can for a successful future."

"You're so thoughtful." He leaned over to kiss her. "Let's take a road trip, and then we'll take the rest of the day off. We'll get a hotel with a pool and let you just lay out and relax."

"It's October," she pointed out stiffly.

"An indoor pool," he modified.

"You're so silly, love. Thank you. I think I'm going to take a nap. Wake me when we get there?"

"I'm going to get us a rental. You can sleep then." He leaned forward in the seat. "Sorry, driver. Change in plans. Take us to the closest place I can pick up a car."

"Hmm. Best place would be the airport," the cabbie replied.

Blake hung his head. "Fine. Airport, then." Leaning back, he grinned at her. "I guess you get a short nap after all."

"Thanks." Blake accepted the keys and shoved the rental agreement in his pocket. Taking Sarah's hand, he led her outside where a plain blue sedan awaited them. Putting her in the passenger side, he cooed, "Don't forget your seatbelt, babe. Would you like a blanket and a pillow?"

"What for?" she asked, giggling as she snapped the device into place.

"I see a dollar store right over there." He pointed at the neon sign with a stiff digit. "It's going to be a longer drive than I thought..." his voice trailed away.

"Oh." She sighed. "Yeah, if you don't mind."

"Not a problem, pumpkin." Blake hopped in, driving the short distance. Leaving her, he dashed in to make the purchase, then handed them to her upon his return. "I already shoved the pillow into a nice case for you, and the blanket is —"

"So soft!" she squealed, cutting him off. Rubbing it against her face, she grinned. "I love it! Thank you." She beamed at him.

"Good. Snuggle up, then. We'll be in Savannah before you know it."

Propping her pillow in the laid-back seat, she only half heard where they were going. Awakening a few hours later, she asked, "Who is in Savannah?"

"Why hello, sunshine!" Blake chuckled at her. "Do we need a pitstop?"

"Yes, please. I swear this baby polka dances on my bladder." She moaned, rubbing the lower part of her belly. "How close are we?"

"Less than an hour, but there's a group of convenience stores just ahead. We'll pick one and have a bite of lunch if you want."

"Sounds good," she replied, shoving her pillow and blanket into the back seat with their bags. Fighting to get her seat upright, she cursed. "I hate these fucking things."

Blake frowned. "Did you sleep well?"

"Yeah, but it's never enough," she complained. "I thought the tired phase should have ended by now."

"Me, too," he mumbled, then added a little louder, "Maybe you aren't resting enough at night."

"No wonder there. As soon as I lay down or get still, this kid goes nuts."

"Aw, honey," he soothed, placing his hand on her belly as she righted the chair. "It won't last forever. And we are going to love this baby so much."

"I know." She sniffled, hiding her tears.

Blake pursed his lips to quell his amusement. "You are such a mess. I love you, princess."

"I love you too," she whispered. Sitting back, she exhaled loudly, then climbed out when they had come to a stop. Dashing, she made it to the toilet just in time.

Blake waited for her outside the door, catching her hand as she came out. "They have a little diner on the other side of the store," he offered. "Let's have a small lunch before we head into town."

"Sounds good," she replied, smiling up at him with clear green eyes. She had splashed cool water on her face to wash away the caked tears from her lashes, leaving her refreshed. "I'm sorry I'm such an emotional mess."

"No worries," he replied, holding out her chair. "You are the light of my life. Be as emotional as you need to be, my sweet."

Enjoying meals of chicken fried steak and mashed potatoes, Sarah was in heaven. "That was so good! They don't serve meals like that in Boston," she praised as they climbed back into their rental.

"They certainly don't," he agreed, giving her a wink. "Are you ready to hear about our trip to Savannah?" He started the engine and pointed them in the right direction.

"Yeah. I think I'm caught up on my sleep. At least for the moment."

"Well, while you were out, I had time to think about things, and I remembered a lot more than I thought I did. We definitely need to visit the book shop on Oak Lane," he suggested.

"A book shop?" She failed to see the significance of dusty old tomes.

"Yes. We've done business with them a few times, trading volumes for special clients," he explained. "We haven't done much lately, but in the past, I think our family was connected to the owners a little more closely."

"Oh." Sarah gasped, then laughed. "I thought you were going to look for my parents' coven. But you're looking for Widow Korrigan."

"Yes," he hissed. "But she isn't a widow. If my hunch is correct, she is my Aunt Abigail. I knew her when I was a kid, and I loved her spirit. Aunt Abby was definitely different."

"How so?" She grinned at him, his excitement obvious. Even if the investigation turned out fruitless, she hoped he enjoyed the trip down memory lane.

"Well, she only called herself a widow so people would

leave her alone. She was actually a spinster, and she liked it that way."

"Like Merideth," Sarah surmised.

"Yeah." He shrugged. "But back then, women weren't allowed to be independent. They got married, had children, and were good little wives. It was all that was expected of them," he concluded. "Almost even all that was allowed."

"And you think this is the same person?" she asked doubtfully.

"Actually, I do, for two reasons. The first is my brother. He was obsessed with Brenna, even when we were kids. One time, Aunt Abby told him that someday Brenna would bring him to a bad end." Blake sneered. "I swear, she was such a talented seer. I think it is an omen. No matter how long the battle, eventually we will win."

"But my would-be parents said she was an old crone. Are you sure they weren't talking about your mother?"

"Haha! No." He glanced at her, his enthused expression giving weight to his words. "My mother would not have protected you. They said you were born, and your birthmark hinted at what would come of it. The old crone convinced them to spirit you away in hopes of avoiding that scenario."

"And your Aunt Abigail wanted to stop it from happening," Sarah whispered. "Why wouldn't my real parents help her?"

"I have no idea." Blake shook his head. "And we may never find out. But for now, at least for today, I think it's worth a look. Maybe my aunt is still around somewhere, and we could talk to her." He beamed at the prospect of finding someone, anyone, from the old family who would take his side. "And of course, we will try to avoid their coven if we can, just in case they are still around as well. Perhaps some aliases might be in order."

"I just use Brenna," she pointed out. "It's easy to remember and pretty much rolls off the tongue."

"I guess I could be Rider," Blake proposed. "Think that would work?"

"Only if you don't talk shit to me," she teased.

Rubbing her belly, Sarah turned to the window. Lost in her own thoughts, she wondered if any of what he searched for would make any difference to them in the end, or if the day were merely a pleasant distraction. "Wow, this place is creepy as fuck," she observed as they pulled up in front of a dated structure.

"I have to agree." Blake stared at the long veranda on the front. "I don't know that I've ever been here. But Savannah is supposed to be the most haunted place in America. Maybe we'll meet a ghost inside."

Sarah grinned. "You're so goofy. I'm sure that just a tourist thing."

"Maybe," he grunted. They still hadn't moved. "We won't know until we go inside," he added, cocking his head to look at her. "Unless you're scared."

Sarah grabbed the latch. "I've faced your brother. With a pistol. I'm not scared of shit." Shoving the door open, she climbed out and mounted the steps.

Yanking the door open, Sarah paused once she was inside. A dusty old book store was the only way to describe it. Her eyes swinging over the sales floor, it reminded her of M & Js before they took over and updated it. When she reached the counter to the right, she noticed a slender woman with dark hair seated on the other side.

"Can I help you?" she asked, closing her book, and laying it on the flat surface before her.

"We're just here to look around," Sarah clipped.

"We?" the girl asked doubtfully, then gasped as Blake stepped through the door.

NINE

Moving On

"Hey, Hannah." Meri walked up to her during a lull in the action. "Mind if I step out for a bit?"

"Not at all!" The blonde beamed at her. "I'm fine, so take your time."

"Great. I'm going to wander over to have a look at our new office." She lowered her chin to her chest, giving her new partner a devious grin.

"Oh, my goodness!" Hanna clapped her hands, bouncing in place. "Does that mean you're ready to get started?"

Merideth swallowed, the thought of moving on still hard to take. "Yeah. It's time we looked at writing our business plan." She held the smile, hoping the other girl couldn't see the cracks in her emotions.

"I'm so excited!" She clapped again. "Take your time. And snap some pictures so we can talk when you get back. I have some ideas, but I don't want to do anything without your agreement."

"You got it." Merideth knocked on the counter, then pushed on the glass door.

"Where's she going?" Rider asked, joining their clerk with coffee in one hand and a jelly filled pastry in the other.

"We're making plans on our new shop," she informed him brightly. "Blake may need to get a move on with the hiring."

"Yeah. I'll be sure to tell him that," Rider clipped, taking a large bite.

Across the store, Ezamay sat in the comfy chairs. Every few minutes she would turn the page on the tome she was reading. Sauntering over to her, Rider sank down in one of the other seats. "Have you decided to join the crew around here?"

"I'm not really cut out for running a business," she explained, not taking her eyes of her book.

"You don't have to run it." He laughed. "You just take their money and put it in the register. Answer a few questions here and there."

"I'm sure there is far more to it than that."

"Well, if you're not here to work, mind if I ask why you came along?" He craned his neck for a better look at what she had in her lap. "Blake's got a collection of really good ones in the basement. Dark curses and some nice charms if you're interested."

She raised her eyes slowly, meeting his. "You wouldn't hurt her, would you?"

Her voice low, he barely heard the words. Staring at her, mouth falling open, he blurted, "Not a chance. Why would you even think that I would?"

"The way that you speak to her. You were overly nice to her when she first ended it, but you are downright hateful these days."

"You get what you give," he replied tartly, breaking the

connection. Finishing off his donut, he chewed it for a minute, then took a swig of coffee to wash it down. "I don't want her getting any ideas."

"What sort of ideas? She has made it clear that there is no reconciliation," Ezamay pointed out. "Let there be peace in our family, Rider."

"Our family?" He coughed, cutting her a cold glare. "You and I aren't related, remember?" It hurt that he would never call her Mom.

"You are the brother of one daughter, and believe it or not, the other still cares very deeply for you." She sniffled, returning to her book. "All I ask is that you allow her to heal," she added quietly.

Watching her, he breathed a heavy sigh. His stubbornness had cost him much over his lifetime. It cut to his core that Meri could be listed as such. "I'll try," he offered. "But I can't promise anything."

Across the street, Merideth strolled up to their new building, nervously rolling the keys in her hand. They were getting the east end, as Blake put it, so she looked up at the morning sun and grinned. Locating the key, she inserted it and gave the handle a twist. "Oh, I love this French door!" she squealed. "I'll repaint it and make it really pop."

Stepping inside, a few shelves and a desk remained. And several boxes of pure junk. "The first thing we need is a trash can." Turning slow circles, she imagined the transformed space.

"We'll need a client table with four chairs over here. Right by the window so the sunlight warms our plants." She used her hands to mockup the arrangement. "And we'll need a few of those folding privacy screens to divide the room when we need to."

Meri smiled genuinely, moving through the area, and making her plans aloud, as if Hannah had joined her. Remembering to take a few pictures, she envisioned each portion of the space. When she reached the back, however, she felt as if she might vomit. "What a foul odor!" She gasped, peeking in at the toilet. Flicking the lights, she realized the electricity was off.

Giving the shop another inspection, she found the breaker box. From there, she realized the electricity had not been reconnected. "Of course. You have to spend some money before you can make some money." Finances would be one of their first conversations, and she felt certain they were going to need a third partner, or in the least a loan. She took a picture of it as well, to remind her to have it reinstated. She also took one of the bathroom, so she could call a plumber about taking care of that smelly situation. "We will definitely need our toilet," she confirmed.

Satisfied with her inspection, Meri let herself out the front, taking care to lock the doors. As she strolled down the walk-in front of the rest of the building, she passed by the windows on Rider's section. Blake had given him the large retail portion, so at some point, she could expect him to set up his new art gallery there.

Unable to resist, she placed her hands on the large picture window, pressing her nose to the glass between them to peer inside. Either the owner of this shop had felt the need to tidy up before they left, or Rider had been working on it. Clean and neat, a few framed pictures leaned against a single wall. In the center of the room, a telephone sat on the floor. Other than that, it appeared empty.

Squinting and looking harder, she could see a door in the back. "What do you know. He has a toilet as well." She felt grateful, as he would have no excuse to borrow theirs.

Dropping her arms and moving to the last section, Meri considered how hard her life would be, at least for a while. Sharing her bathroom at home with her ex had been difficult enough. Working next door to him for the rest of her life seemed unbearable. But that would be the great thing about having Hannah as a partner. At some point, she hoped they would move up, and leave this small office behind.

Glancing in at Joseline's portion, she could see why it was given to her. The retail space consisted of a shadowbox style window in the front, so she could display her wares, but the rest of the room was obviously intended as workspace. "I wonder what kind of shop this was?"

"A florist," a voice replied, taking Merideth by surprise.

Looking around, she found a short, gray-haired man next to her. "I see." Meri breathed, not sure what to think about his being there. "Are you sure?" she asked, scrunching her nose at the window once more.

"Quite certain. They put display arrangements in these boxes. If you look up, you can see the extra ventilation above them. They weren't refrigerated, but they were kept cooler than the rest of the room," he explained.

"Oh, that will be perfect for Joseline's candles. They won't melt, even with the sun," she observed.

"And Joseline is?"

"My sister. She is getting this end, while my partner and I are taking the other. Her brother is taking the center, for his art studio," she explained briefly, not seeing the harm in sharing.

"It will be nice to see this old place up and running again," the man replied, giving her a nod as he moved along, exiting by the far end and continuing down the road.

"Yes, it will," she agreed as he disappeared out of sight. She darted across the street a minute later, her resolve renewed and ready to share her plans. Bursting through the glass door, she noted the floor remained calm. "Good. Things didn't get out of hand."

Still seated with Ezamay, Rider also turned the pages of a book, making him appear to be a guest rather than an employee. "Did he help with anything while I was gone?" she snipped while scrolling the pictures she had just taken.

"He helped make fresh coffee," Hannah offered. "But I'm pretty sure it was because he wanted some."

"No doubt." Meri snickered.

"I'm sorry things are bad between you," Hannah offered.

"They aren't bad," Merideth denied, her eyes snapping up to meet the cool green ones of the other girl.

"They look bad from here," the blonde offered, laying her hand over Merideth's. "If you ever need to talk, I'm here. And I'm discreet."

Pressing her lips together, Meri muted the trembling of the bottom one. "I appreciate that. We will be working together closely, so it's important that we have each other's best interest at heart." She laid her free hand over hers, creating a stack, then paused as her head swam. Images flying at her, she inhaled sharply. "Oh, Hannah," she breathed.

"Oh my gosh, am I getting a reading?" She grinned, excited at the prospect.

"I don't do readings," Merideth denied, pulling her appendages away.

"But I saw you. You know something," Hannah insisted. "I've seen Auntie do it too many times not to know what that look means."

"I'm opening an interior design business, not a fortune telling booth," the older woman clipped, returning to the photos on her device. "I think this will be a great location for the client table," she began, ready to give her partner the tour.

Pursing her lips, Hannah reluctantly agreed to drop the subject. But deep down, she knew her friend had seen something. Perhaps something dark, making it difficult to share. At some point she hoped her new partner would open up, and that there would be no, or few, secrets between them.

TEN

Nothing to See Here

"Judoc Korrigan!" Her dark hair shimmered as the clerk got to her feet. Coming around the counter, she splayed her fingers across his chest, as if feeling for his heartbeat. "I knew you would come," she whispered.

Dropping him, she grabbed the door, quickly locking it, and drawing the shade. Flipping the sign in the window, she hissed, "We must hurry. And hope that no one has seen."

"Seen what?" Sarah snapped. "We're from out of town. Who the hell would expect us to be here?"

"Sarah," Blake cautioned, studying their host. "You have used my name. You are obviously a powerful seer," he allowed. "But I have little use for such talents."

"You have no faith in our gifts. I understand." The woman took his hand. "You have suffered great loss. And found great strength." She cut her dark eyes over at Sarah. "I'm Loren, by the way." She pulled at him. "Come. Sit at my table, that I may serve you."

Sarah rolled her eyes, following the pair as the girl led them down a long hallway. "Wow. This looks familiar," she groused when they entered a back chamber. Simple wooden chairs for clients greeted them, with a larger bench covered in pillows against the wall. Between them, a rickety table topped with a large crystal ball.

The girl released her target, offering him a seat. Then she plucked one of the pillows and held it out. "For you, Madam."

Slowly, Sarah extended her hands to accept it. Their eyes locked, she studied the witch. "How did you know we would come here?"

"So much of your path is marked, Sarah Matthews. Please, sit." Her hair floated slightly as she spun, facing Blake. "You are star crossed lovers, as they say. Your fate is uncertain, and you seek insight for the fight that lies before you."

Sarah stared at her, then rested her hand on her belly. She considered sitting on the cushion, then placed it behind her to lean against. "Oh, that feels good," she whispered, the ache in her back relieved by the support it provided. "Thank you."

"You are very welcome." Loren bowed her head slightly towards her. Then she turned again to Blake, who had remained silent, his eyes watching around them. "Magister," she addressed him, and his gaze snapped to her.

"You obviously hold great talent," he repeated. "But I must warn you, I place little merit in the words of the seer." He chuckled. "We have not had great luck with them in the past, I'm afraid."

"Your stubbornness clouds your understanding," she observed. "The words of the seer are seldom wrong, Judoc."

"Blake, please," he corrected, his lips puckering. "All right, have your say," he commanded, his hand raised towards her device. He saw nothing inside it, as usual, but perhaps this time what the mystic saw would make sense.

"You mock me," she clipped. "Why have you come into my store. You obviously find nothing to see here."

"Ah, I was looking for a book, actually." He grinned at her, humoring her.

"A book? And what would you find between the musty pages? Answers you seek sprinkled among the dust," she snapped.

"Well, at least the truth would be there. Written clearly for all to read." Blake stared at her, his heart pounding in his chest. She appeared odd to him, as if caught in a trance, her eyes no longer seeing him. Her ears no longer hearing his denial. "Loren?"

"Yes." She continued, her words tumbling out of her thin lips. "But the truth is seldom clear, written though it may be."

"Oh, shit." He gasped, sinking into her daze with her.

"Blake –" Sarah began, but his hand shot up, stopping her.

"Shh. Listen." His eyes fixed on the mouth as it moved, he allowed her words to tumble over him. To seep into his very being.

"You, who are caught in a battle never lost but cannot be won. Brother against brother, father against son. The girl you both desire, and the child you each hold at stake. A babe with a future uncertain, and a path you fear to take."

"Yes," Blake hissed.

"Your numbers are great, the count among you grows. But forces that stand against you must be equal, clinging to their shadows," she recited.

Sarah stared at her, then cut her eyes over to Blake. As the woman spoke, his lips moved, as if they repeated what she had just said. Listening, her brow scrunched. She had never seen him like this, and it struck fear into her very core.

"Do not take your counsel for granted. Do not give your

company your hate. For it is in the light of friendship and love that a blessed future will make." She blinked rapidly, then raised her hand to her crystal ball. "Now, do you wish for a reading or not?"

Blake coughed, the words still turning in his mind.

"Is that not what you just gave us?" Sarah asked, perplexed.

"It's fine," Blake cautioned. "Tell us about my Aunt Abby. Where may we find her?" he added quickly.

"She still walks among the living, though many years have tested her resolve. You wish to count her as an ally, but she has not chosen a side in your quest," Loren observed.

"What is going on here?" Sarah demanded, totally baffled.

"Just go with it," Blake commanded. "I'll explain in the car." Glancing at their host, he indicated her with a stiff palm. "Ask her anything you like."

"I doubt she would give an answer anyone would understand," Sarah grunted, crossing her arms and resting them atop her belly.

"Precisely." Blake grinned, glancing at his watch. "Oh, my. Look at the time." Standing, he proposed, "Perhaps we should call it a day, sweetheart. We do have a bit of a drive back to Atlanta."

"You do not wish to hear more?" Loren asked, gazing up at him.

"I think I've heard quite enough, actually." Using Sarah's arm, he practically dragged her to her feet. "We'll just be going now. Thank you for a lovely reading." He opened his wallet, dropping a hundred on the table, then shoving his girlfriend towards the door.

Outside, the sun had moved to the west. "Wow," Sarah observed. "It's like we were in there for hours."

"Yeah. It felt that way to me as well. Get in and we'll get out of here," he instructed, opening her door for her.

Behind the wheel, Blake didn't look back. Massaging his lips, he appeared deep in thought. "Do you have something to write on?" he asked suddenly. "Check the glove box."

She opened it. "Just an owner's manual and some advertisements," she informed him. Laying her seat back, she added, "But, I have a diary in my bag. We can use that." Rolling onto her knees, she fought for balance as he weaved through the traffic. "Gees. This is fun."

"You keep a diary?" he asked in surprise.

"Doesn't everyone?" she replied tartly.

"I don't," he confessed, imagining how thick such a book would be.

Locating the small brown tome, she snagged the pen as well. Righting herself in the seat, she adjusted the back. "There we go. What am I writing?"

"What she said. Loren. We need to put it all down before we forget it," he suggested.

"But it was all gibberish. Fathers and brothers. Being scared to take a walk. Nonsense," she complained. Flipping to a blank page at the back, she sighed.

"No, it was exactly what we need to know. It's so clear, but hazy. Like hidden in a fog. All we have to do is riddle it out," he explained glancing at her.

"Ok, I get it. Tell me what to write."

"Well, she said a girl we were both fighting over. Obviously you. And she said brother against brother," he recalled.

"You and Morcant." She added bullet points, jotting down two lines. "What else?"

"I need you to help me remember, Sarah. There was something in the rhythm of the words. Like a song or a chant." He glanced at her. "Can you try."

She sighed heavily, then closed her eyes. "Your numbers are great, the count among you grows."

"Yes!" he nearly shouted. "Write that down. The next line is, but forces that stand against you must be equal, clinging to their shadows."

Sarah stared at her page, the words blurring. "I feel weird."

"It's ok, pumpkin. Look out the window so you don't get carsick." He licked at his lips anxiously, then added, "What else did she say?"

Sarah scratched a few more words on the page, then read them back to him. "Do not take your counsel for granted. Do not give your company your hate. For it is in the light of friendship and love that a blessed future make."

"Yes, she said that at the end," Blake agreed. "But there was more. I wish I could remember it all."

"I find when I'm struggling, it's like the memory hides. Relax and it will come to you."

Blake closed his eyes.

"Hey! You're driving, remember?"

He peeked at her with one eye. "The traffic is light. Do you want to find a hotel?" he asked, indicating the setting sun.

"Let's just get back to Atlanta. I don't want to spend the night at some podunk dive in the middle of nowhere."

Blake snapped his fingers. "It's a babe with a future uncertain and a path you fear to take." He tapped her page. "Write that down."

"Are you sure?"

"Yes. Madam Demore said the same thing when I asked her about the baby," he confessed.

"She said it was a path you feared to take?" Sarah sniffled, the idea of it tearing at her heart.

"No. She said the baby's future was uncertain. That's why I didn't want to tell you about the reading."

"But if they both said the same thing, maybe it's true." She ran her hand across her belly. "What if our baby is in danger?"

"I think we're all in danger, love. We are in a battle that is never lost but cannot be won. She said that, too." He twisted his neck, causing it to crackle. "Brother against brother, father against son."

Sarah used her pen to underline words in the passage. "I think you're right about the song. A lot of these lines rhyme if you put them in the right order."

"That was the most amazing reading I have ever experience," he confessed.

"You were really into it," she observed. "It was pretty creepy to watch, actually."

"I'm sorry it frightened you, sweet pea. I just got caught up in it. Like everything was so clear. Now it's all muddled again."

"Lost in the shadows. I wonder if we are lost, or they are," Sarah pondered.

"Yeah, with that thing about our numbers being equal. I think it means his are hiding from us," Blake proposed.

Scratching the last line, she offered, "I'll tear this out for you, and you can think it over for a few days."

"No, don't!" he screamed, preventing her mutilation of the page. "It's a book, get it?" He grinned, his excitement at fever pitch despite her squinted glare.

"This is my diary," she replied curtly, indicating the words trespassing in her private space.

"What, are you afraid I'm going to read the rest of it?" he teased.

"No, but it's…private. I'd like to keep it that way."

"Well, don't take it out," he said, desperate to prevent the removal. "The answers we seek are sprinkled within the pages. That's what she said. The truth is there, written clearly for all to see. Please don't take it out," he finished at nearly a whisper.

Sarah blinked at him. "You really think this is something."

"I know that it is. Of all the mystics I have visited, Merideth has been the clearest. Until today."

"Meri? I didn't think she was that great, to be honest," Sarah clipped, closing the book and pushing it between her legs for safe keeping.

"Oh, our girl is a gifted witch, ladybug. I'm so glad she's on our side." He tapped his fingers on the wheel, thinking of her. "Do you know why she refuses to marry Rider?"

"Because he's a misogynistic asshole?" Sarah coughed a sharp laugh. "He'd have her barefoot and pregnant in the kitchen in no time."

"No. And he's not, I don't think. He just takes getting used to." He grinned at her observation. "No, she is fighting it because she knows they are meant to be together. She is flat refusing to admit the truth."

"How are you so certain?" She looked over at her mate wistfully. "I thought you weren't a seer."

"I'm not. I'm the witch whisperer, remember?" He chuckled. "I can tell when a witch has been casting or using magic. When they came into the shop, she was dripping with the craft. But he didn't have a speck on him."

"What does that prove?" She shrugged.

"Secret sister or not, they were kismet. They would never have been together, otherwise. I didn't need any special sight to know that," he bragged. "I wonder if they are the star-crossed lovers."

"Oh, I forgot she said that." Sarah pulled the book out of her lap and scribbled in the line. "I'll keep this safe for you, baby."

"Thanks, kitten," he purred, reaching for her hand. "It's dark, can we stop now?"

"Sure," she agreed. "We'll get some sleep and an early start. Be at the airport in time for our flight home."

"Sounds like a plan." He set the blinker and took the next exit, looking forward for a little hotel sex before he drifted off to sleep.

ELEVEN

Enough Yesterday

RISING EARLY AGAIN ON THURSDAY, Meri dragged her weary self into the bathroom and locked Rider's side of the door. "I'm first today," she growled, leaving the bathroom to start her coffee.

He banged on the portal a minute later. "Are you even in there?" he shouted from the other side.

"Yes, I'm on the toilet. Do you mind?" she hollered back, grinning as she poured her cup.

"I bet," he snarled. "Fine." He pulled a pair of pants over his boxers and marched to the kitchen to start his morning brew. To his surprise, Ezamay had already done so. "You're up early," he observed.

"I thought I might get ahead of the door slamming," she joked. Tapping the side of her mug with her fingers, she waited for the fresh stream to end. "And I returned the favor." She held up her hand to indicate the coffee dripping into the carafe.

"Thank you. That was very thoughtful." He ran his hand roughly across the back of his neck. "Merideth got in the bathroom before of me," he explained.

"I guess she wanted to get ahead of the slamming as well." May smiled at him deviously.

"I guess she did." Rider coughed a short laugh. "She's pretty tenacious."

"Oh, certainly. I believe that stubborn streak is about the only thing the two of you ever had in common."

"What do you mean?" he demanded, standing straight to face her as the pot finished and she poured her cup.

Taking a seat at the table, she waited for him to join her. "You were always at odds," she explained when he had done so. "Polar opposites. If she wanted red, you wanted blue."

Rider made a face, not sure red and blue would be considered opposites.

"If you were hot, she was cold," Ezamay elaborated.

"Ah." He nodded. "We weren't on the same page." He took a noisy sip. "Too bad you missed the show the day I proposed."

"Yes. What a terrible time for a nap!" She laughed, considering it. "I guess it must have been rather painful."

"Excruciating," he confessed, swirling his cup. "She didn't do it on purpose. I know deep down I should have taken Blake's advice and waited."

"Do you think the outcome would have been any different?"

"Pfft, no. I don't think she was ever going to say yes. At least this way I can let go and move on with my life," he observed.

"Oh, Rider." She cackled. "It doesn't look like that's what you're doing from here." She drank the last of her cup and placed it in the sink. "I'd like to ride with you again today. How long do I have?"

"How long do you need?" he asked, blinking up at her.

"I'm not sure. Perhaps you'll simply wait for me?" she suggested as she sauntered out the door.

"Crochety old woman," he muttered, returning to his coffee. "She knows exactly what she's doing." Getting on to him for rushing Merideth yesterday. But subtle. Sneaky, so he feels bad and she doesn't come off heavy handed. Pushing the chair back, he poured another cup and headed to his room.

When he arrived, he could at least hear the shower running. Taking a seat on a stool before one of his paintings, he stared at the non-invasive rosebush that held the center, then heaved a loud sigh. He had strolled the garden, taking shots of Blake's collection of flora. They weren't much, but they had gotten him started. Opening a tube of paint, he dabbed a small amount on his pallet, then used a brush to apply it.

Behind him, the water ended. "That was quick." He'd expected her to use every drop. A few minutes later, the lock was released on the door.

"It's your turn," her voice called through the crack.

For the first time in months, he felt the urge to paint. Almost to the point of handing the two women the keys to his little green car and sending them away. Deciding against it, he set aside his paraphernalia and wandered into the bathroom, in no real hurry to face the day.

When Rider finally exited his room, both Merideth and Ezamay sat in the living room, waiting on him. "Are we ready?"When he got closer, he noticed Merideth swipe away tears. "What's the matter?"

"Nothing," she snapped, gathering her purse and heading to the door.

"I'm selling my house," Ezamay announced. "I've decided I've had enough of yesterday. Too many memories of my husband there, and it's time I made a new start."

"Are you going to live here in Boston?" he asked, locking the door as the girls climbed into his car. Watching Meri get into the back seat, it occurred to him that he had purchased the vehicle for her. If he'd gotten the car he wanted, a mint green VW bug wouldn't have been it. Looking down at the keys, he was taken with the notion to simply give it to her and buy another one.

"I believe that I am," Ezamay stated calmly as he started the car.

Behind him, Merideth took a ragged breath. Saying nothing, her emotions ran high, in full view, so she didn't have to. Deciding against making a decision on the car, at least for today, he shifted the gear and drove them to the store in silence.

"Yeah!" Karen shouted, running up to give Sarah a hug. "I'm so glad to see you guys!"

"We've been here a while," Blake pointed out from his seat.

"And we have so much to share," Sarah added, giving her best friend a squeeze.

"Like what," Joseline asked, picking up on Sarah's vibe.

Turning to her bag, the girl fished out her diary. "I have it all written down." She wafted the book at them.

"Is that your journal?" Karen gasped. "I would say it was private."

"We didn't have anything else to write on," Blake pointed out sarcastically. "The last few pages have the list."

"The list," Sarah mocked. "That's one way of putting it."

Joseline pursed her lips. "You guys are so cryptic. Just spit it out. List of what?" she asked, afraid they had thought of additions for their wedding. Only a few weeks away, there would be no way to accommodate them.

"We more or less visited a mystic," Blake confessed. "Only this one gave me chills."

"She gave him more than that! He was practically in a trance listening to her," Sarah pointed out. Locating the page, she skimmed down it. The words she had circled and underlined leapt out at her. "There's a lot to unpack here."

"Well, read or hand it over," Karen instructed, holding out her hand to accept the tome.

Deciding to do so, Sarah used the band of elastic to tackdown the pages that came before their list. The private ones. "Go on. See what you make of them."

Taking adjacent empty seats, Jos and Karen shared the pages between them. Leaning their heads together, they read, then whispered and pointed. When they were done, Karen closed the journal and handed it back.

"She said all of those things to you?" Josee asked doubtfully.

"Yes. It was like a song or chant tumbling out of her," Blake explained. "I've never seen anything like it."

"Some of it is pretty spot on, but other parts harder to discern. Brother against brother is easy, but father against son?" Karen pointed out.

"I'm afraid that's Rider and Thaddeus," Blake predicted. "His old man is probably supporting Morcant, as we suspected before Rider joined us."

"Great. So he's one of the forces in the shadows?" Karen asked, standing as the attendant called for their plane to board.

"If he is, there are a lot more of them we don't know." Sarah sighed.

"Why do you think that?" Joseline put her bag over her shoulder to follow her.

"It says our numbers are equal. If we have six, they have six, which means there are at least five more we don't know about. Somewhere," Blake supplied, joining them.

"Like I said, it's a lot to unpack. It may take us days to figure it all out." Sarah brought up the rear, glad Blake had hoisted her bag for her. Holding her belly, she felt as if she carried a load everywhere she went, and she still had three months to the day before she was due.

When the group landed in Boston a few hours later, Blake announced, "Lets stop and get an early dinner. Then I can drop Sarah off at the house before I head up to the store."

"No way," Sarah squealed. "I want to see how it went, too. Besides, I want to make a copy of the mystic list for everyone." The thought of sharing her journal with the others made her cringe, so handing copies out to each seemed like a decent fix.

"Why don't you just tear them out and share them?" Joseline asked as she climbed into the back seat of his car.

"Because Blake is superstitions," Sarah informed them with a twisted grin.

"I am not," he denied. Placing the bags in the trunk, he slammed the lid. Sliding behind the wheel, he shook his head at her.

"That doesn't tell us anything," Karen pointed out with an upturned palm. "Why can't we tear them out?"

Blake sighed, hitting the button to start his car. "Just something Loren and I agreed upon. The words written in a book for all to see, or something like that."

"Loren is your mystic?" Joseline asked, glancing between them.

"Yeah. She was creepy. And her place was more like a

worn down, has-been shop." Sarah shivered. "I'm glad we updated ours."

"Commercialized," Blake added. "Loren's shop was primitive. She did have a cool reading room though."

"Well, if you can't tear them out, then make us the copies," Joseline agreed. "I love puzzles. I'd love to take a crack at that one."

Blake watched her in the rear-view mirror for a moment, then nodded. "I think some of it will come easy, but if it's like most things given by a seer, it won't mean what we think it does."

"It'll be fine," Karen pointed out. "It gives us more than we had. Let's get that lunch. I'm starving."

Choosing a place that would be fast and convenient, the quartet piled out of the car and strolled inside.

"Do you think everything went all right at the store?" Joseline asked when they were seated with their meals. She hadn't given it much thought while they were away, but the closer they got to home, the more anxious she became. "Rider and Meri haven't been getting along that great."

"Yeah, that's an understatement." Blake ate a few fries, considering the issue. "I'm not typically one to meddle. And he has totally ignored the advice that I have given. But what if we tried to help them get back together?" he suggested calmly.

"To what end?" Joseline snapped. "They clearly want different things. If anything, we should work on keeping them apart. Helping them get on with their lives *separately*."

"I've got a friend I could introduce Rider to," Sarah suggested. "But he's kind of a dick, so I don't know if I would want to do that to her."

"Hey!" Jos snapped. "He's still my brother."

"And dicks need girlfriends, too," Blake quipped, popping another chunk of potato.

"Cute," Karen observed, glancing at Jos and thinking of her dildo collection with a snicker. Joseline giggled, following her train of thought when their eyes met.

"I guess that's an inside joke," Sarah observed. "I need more ketchup." She scooted out of her seat to help herself at the condiment bar. When she returned, she observed, "Actually, I know a guy that might suit Merideth. He's all uptight, like she is."

"Are you saying our seer is stiff?" Blake jeered.

"I'm saying, she's a bit staunchy. Prim and proper. I can't even imagine what that must be like in bed." The group laughed at Sarah's observation.

"I don't ever plan to find out," Blake added, giving his girl a wink.

"So, what are we going to do? *Nothing* sounds like a good idea to me." Joseline gave her opinion firmly.

"It wouldn't hurt to introduce Meri to someone," Blake said thoughtfully. "It's not really meddling. I mean, they have to start seeing other people at some point. Maybe it will help speed the process."

"And they can stop being so cruel to each other and just get on with it," Karen agreed.

"I'll call him," Sarah confirmed. "I think I still have his number."

"Great." Joseline rolled her eyes and reached for her shake, wondering why her friends couldn't just leave well enough alone.

TWELVE

Yet to Come

WALKING HER TO THE DOOR, Albert held Merideth's arm gently. "Wow, I have to admit, for a blind date that wasn't so bad."

"I was just thinking the same thing," she replied crisply, pausing on the bottom step. Looking up at the entrance, she cringed. "But we can't go in there."

"I...heard." He let her off the hook. "Your ex lives here as well."

"In the same building, yes." Her eyes wide, she gasped. "Would you like to come in for coffee? We can go around to the back and it's only ten feet from there to my door."

"Look, Meri." He waved a hand at her. "I'm not a sex on the first date kind of guy."

Hot flush instantly crept up her neck to her cheeks. "I should say not."

Seeing that he had embarrassed her, he stopped there. "You really meant coffee, didn't you?"

"I have a small pot in my room," her voice squeaked. "But if you want to wait for the second date before you see my little apartment, I'm fine with that too."

"How long does it take to see your bed? Realistically?"

She felt as if she were being judged. "You can see it from the kitchen," she clipped. "Getting into it might take a while."

"Then I'll wait." Stepping forward, her height matched him perfect, and he kissed her on the cheek. "I really like you," he whispered. "Not bad for a blind date." Turning on his heel, he strolled back to his car and climbed inside. A moment later, he was gone.

"Oh my gosh," she whispered, holding her chest with one hand, and the place his lips had brushed with the other. Grinning ear to ear, she clomped up the remaining steps and rushed inside. In the kitchen, she opened the fridge and stared at the selection.

"Did you have a nice time?" Ezamay asked from the doorway. Judging by the clock, she doubted it.

"Oh, Mother, it was wonderful. We talked about so many things. Everything. Nothing." She claimed a bottle of wine and selected a glass. "Sit with me?"

"I'll have a snort," Ezamay agreed, shaking her head. "Do you want to tell me about him, or just sit and ramble a bit?"

Placing a second glass on the table, Merideth poured each half full. "Either. Both. I don't know." She shook her hair in giddy delight.

"Well, maybe you did have a nice time." Taking crystal, May sat, waiting for her daughter to take the other chair.

Lifting the other glass, Merideth hesitated. Taping the crystal with a nail, she considered her words carefully. "I think I need to go to my room. I'd like to be alone."

"Ah. Of course, dear. I'll see you in the morning." No sooner had she gone when Rider appeared.

"Drinking alone?" He pulled a crystal from the rack. "That's the first sign of an alcoholic." Taking the bottle, he helped himself to a glass, then a chair. "I'm going to give Merideth my car," he announced without preamble.

"What? Why?" Ezamay gasped.

"I bought it for her. I wanted to tell her the other morning, but she was so upset about you selling your house, I thought better of it. Maybe you can help me break it to her," he suggested.

"Break it to her, I think she'll be thrilled." Ezamay narrowed her eyes at him. "Why would you do this? Was it promised to her?"

"No, but it's hers." He rubbed his forehead, gathering his thoughts. "Like I said, I bought it with her in mind. The fact that we broke up afterwards is my fault. Besides, my flat in New Orleans sold. I'll be collecting a fair amount from that in a matter of weeks. It's the right thing to do," he finished with a huff.

"Were you aware she had a date tonight?" May asked, sipping her beverage.

"She's on a date?" He looked up at her, his expression unchanged. Then a smile flitted across his lips. "Well, go Meri." He took a large gulp from his glass. "I'll be sure not to disturb them if she brings him home." The smile grew as he recalled her views on friend sex.

"It doesn't upset you?" the older woman pushed.

"No. I can't fix us. And my anger has only led to remorse. Our friendship is all but destroyed. If I could get that much back, I'd be happy," he confessed. "I'm going to be nicer to her if I can, Ezamay. Civil. No reason. No payment required. I want her to be happy, after all, and I only recently discovered how deeply I've been hurting her."

"Are you drunk?" she asked curtly. "How many bottles have you had tonight?"

He laughed loudly, then finished off his glass. "Just the

one I have shared with you." Standing, he leaned over her, kissing her on the forehead. "I'll make sure we are quiet in the morning. And help me decide on the car. I'd like to present it to her soon. Keep her off that damned bus."

"Good night, Rider," she called after him as he wandered towards his hall.

"Well, Rider sure has been behaving strangely," Sarah observed as Merideth helped her with her dress. "I heard he gave you his car."

"Yes, he gave me the keys last night. I still don't know what to think about it." Meri shook her head vigorously. "He said he bought it for me to begin with, if you can believe that." She turned her, pushing and pulling at the seams. "I think it looks good."

"I want to put your hair up," Karen suggested, mussing with the red locks.

"Oh, I don't know," Sarah whined. "Do we have time?"

"Loads," Joseline pointed out. "The ceremony is at eleven, we eat at twelve, and everyone is gone by two."

"That's not much of a reception," Hannah complained. "After all the work we've put into this thing."

"I'll just be happy when it's over," Sarah huffed, blowing loose hairs out of her face. "Ok, put it up." She plunked into a chair, giving the other woman access.

"How about a swoop. Half up," Merideth suggested. They were using her room, for its access to the back and to keep her out of Blake's sight, as some traditions were worth upholding. "I've got pins if you need them."

"Great. Get those and I'll get started." Karen smiled at her best friend, leaning in to whisper. "Don't rush this, love.

We did all this work to give you a wonderful day. It's our gift."

Sarah smiled at her. "I know. Thank you." She cast a glance around at the others. "Thank you all." Noticing Karen still wore her jeans, she scowled. "Did your dress not fit?"

"No, I tried it. It fits fine. All I have to do is slip into it, slide on the shoes, and off we go."

A knock sounded at the door. Merideth opened it a crack, then noticed it was Rider. "Yes?" she clipped, still unsure where they stood. Holding the portal firm, she only allowed him a few inches of access.

"Uhh, Sarah's parents are here," he announced.

"What?" The girl pivoted in the chair to glare at him. "Why?"

"I haven't the foggiest," he claimed with a shrug. "Blake says he invited them, but he's shocked as shit that they showed up. Your dad thinks you need walked down the aisle."

"Tell him thanks but no thanks." She glanced at Meri. "I don't need a man to give me permission to get married. I'm going to walk myself down the aisle."

"You go, girl," Joseline cheered.

"Ok. I'll tell him," Rider agreed as Meri closed the crack.

The girls giggled when he was gone, and Sarah huffed a few deep breaths. "I can do this." She rubbed her belly. "We can do this."

"You know we are here for you," Joseline stated firmly.

A few minutes later, the hair was done with the veil in place, and there was nothing left but the wait. Putting on her dress, Karen examined herself in the full-length mirror propped up beside the wardrobe. "I do like this green, Sarah. I may have to invent a few other occasions to wear it."

"Glad to hear it." Sarah gave her gown a twirl as she

sidled up next to her. Side by side, she leaned against her best friend. "I never dreamed it would be like this. But here we are."

"I'll go see how we're doing with the guests," Joseline offered, slipping out through the bathroom so there was no chance of being seen.

"Are you nervous," Meri asked, fluffing her skirt.

"No. I mean I am at being out there, in front of everyone. But not about getting married." Sarah grinned at her reflection. "It feels right, you know? Like having this baby. Providence." She glanced at Karen, bumping her hip. "I didn't use your word."

Karen giggled. "It would have been all right if you had."

"Everything's in place," Joseline announced as she rejoined them. "When Sarah's ready, we go out through this back door here, and we are good to go."

"How did my dad take the news?" Sarah asked, pulling her veil over her face. "Where's my bouquet?" She twisted around, searching.

"Here's the bouquet." Hannah placed it in her hands.

"Your dad is fine, I guess. He's sitting in a chair with everyone else," Josee reported.

"Good. I hope that means we won't have a scene. Let's do this, ladies!" Sarah smiled at her reflection, then led the way out through Meri's kitchen. Lining up against the wall, those not in the ceremony went out first to get the music started.

Once the procession was ready, being only the two of them, Karen began walking calmly in her beautiful dress. Her smile broad, she couldn't believe they had made it. So many obstacles they had to overcome. So many more in their way. But those didn't matter at that moment, because this was Sarah's big day.

Following behind her, Sarah blew hot air through her lips.

The weather warm for October, she was suddenly grateful they had gotten her hair off her neck. Pausing at the back of the aisle, she shifted her gaze across the few dozen chairs on either side, almost all of them taken. At the front, the arch Merideth had chosen stood looming. To the side of it, Blake waited for her.

Shaking her head, Sarah smiled at the sight of him, as that was all she needed to know. He would be there when she reached the end. The music began, and she marched in time to it, swishing her dress as she moved. Her belly bulged, and she covered a wild kick that sent the light material up in a small plume.

A few more steps, and she could feel the tears on her cheeks, the joy more than she could hold. Arriving at her position, she looked up into her lover's clear blue eyes.

Taking her hands in his, Blake faced his bride. Calmly, coolly, they recited their vows. Lifting her veil, he placed his mouth over hers, and then he laughed for a brief moment, whispering, "And the best is yet to come."

THIRTEEN

Like Father Like Son

AFTER THE CEREMONY, Blake hovered near the back of the house. Enjoying a smoke and a glass of wine, he watched their guests laughing, talking, and dancing. Meanwhile his bride bounced around in her lovely seafoam gown, speaking to different groups of people. Occasionally she twirled, forcing her light, lacy skirt into a float and bringing a proud grin to the groom's lips. A few times, she cupped her belly to show off her bump, which gave him shivers of joy.

"What an amazing day," he mumbled to himself. Sauntering over to the refreshments, Blake poured himself another glass. Taking a sip, he noticed a man in a dark suit come around the far end of the dwelling. In his hand, he carried a large black suitcase. "What the hell is this," he muttered, strolling over to head him off.

When Blake was but a few feet away, he noticed a small boy following behind the gentleman. His hair had been combed smooth, but the waves in his black locks lingered. When their gazes met, Blake noticed that his eyes were a piercing, crystal blue, and he knew instantly there was only one person this child could be. Closing the distance in a few long strides, he stopped the man, preventing him from further invading their privacy. "That's far enough."

"Judoc Korrigan?"

"Yes, I am, but we're celebrating." Holding up his hands, he indicated they should step aside, away from the party.

"Mr. Korrigan, I'm here to deliver –"

"Please." Blake cut him off. "I have guests."

"All well and good, but I have been instructed." The stiff courier handed Blake a simple, plain white envelope. "Upon his mother's death, I am to deliver this letter and this child to you."

Blake stared at the boy. "Do you know who I am?" he asked curtly.

"Yes," the boy replied meekly, blinking up at him.

"Good." Blake knelt next to his small frame. Placing one hand on his back, and the other on his belly, he turned him for a proper view of the bride. "You see that lady? This is her special day, and we don't want anything to ruin it. Tomorrow, we can settle our affairs, but today you must remain quiet. Out of sight. Do you understand?"

"Yes, Father." The boy nodded firmly.

Blake stiffened, then looked up at the delivery man. "You've achieved your goal. You may go."

"Very well." He turned without another word, placing the bag on the ground, and leaving the happy occasion behind him.

"Do you have a name? Or should I call you boy?" Blake smiled briefly at his son, giving him a pat on his small chest.

"Matthew," he stated boldly.

"And how old are you, Matthew?"

"Seven." His tiny lip trembled, showing his first sign of weakness.

A few feet away, Blake noticed Merideth sipping a drink. "Meri," he called to her.

Turning slowly, she stared at him, then picked her way through the grass in her heels to join him. "Who is this?" she asked, giving the young man a gentle pat on the head.

"This is Matthew." Blake stretched to stand beside her. "He is my special guest."

"Guest?" She looked up at him in wonder.

"Yes. Please take him inside and keep him out of the way."

"All right," she replied faintly. Offering her hand, tiny fingers clasped hers, and she gasped. Vivid images flooded her mind, and her eyes snapped to meet Blake's cool blue orbs.

"Please, Meri," Blake hissed. He indicated Sarah, twirling in her lovely gown. "This is her day and I do not wish to see it spoiled. Just care for him, and we will deal with this tomorrow."

"Deal with this," she replied hotly, but he held up his hand, stopping her with his pleading expression. "Ok," she stammered, glancing down at Matt's upturned face. "I'll figure something out."

"Thank you, Merideth." Blake gave her arm a squeeze, then disappeared into the crowd gathered at the refreshment table.

Looking around, Meri spied Rider alone a short distance away. Picking up the suitcase, she guided her charge towards him. "Rider," she said in a hushed tone.

Turning, he faced her, giving her a puzzled look. "You haven't had anything to say to me in weeks and now you want to talk?"

"No. But I need you." Her eyes desperate, she added, "Please."

Looking her up and down, he noticed the boy. Spying the suitcase in her hand, he demanded, "Where are you going?"

"It's his," she clipped. Turning, she led the boy with short quick strides, around the way they had come and into the house via the front door.

Close on her heels, Rider caught her in the front room. "Who is this kid?" he nearly shouted.

"Shh!" she hissed, turning to face him. Her eyes darting around, she listened to the silence of the structure, growing confident everyone was outside. Her eyes landing on the downstairs bathroom, she hoped there was no one in it. "This is Blake's son," she whispered.

"His son!" Rider took a step back in dismay. "Does Sarah know about this?"

"I doubt anyone does. He asked me to keep him quiet and out of the way. He said we would deal with it tomorrow," she explained, glancing down at the familiar features. She adjusted her grip on his hand, smiling at him. "It will be fine, Matthew. This is Rider. We're going to eat some lunch. Are you hungry?"

The boy nodded vigorously, giving her the faintest of grins.

"Holy shit," Rider breathed. "We can't just hide him!"

"Yes, we can," she countered, glancing around once more. Looking up at her ex sternly, she held up the suitcase. "Can you put this in my room and join us in the kitchen?"

Snatching the bag, he groused, "Sure. I'd be glad to." Marching off towards their hallway, he grumbled to himself.

Watching him go, Merideth sighed. Giving the small hand a squeeze, she squared her shoulders and led him towards the kitchen. "Let's see what we can find in here to eat."

Dropping the bag inside Meri's door, Rider sighed. He had promised to be nicer to her, but this was pushing it.

Stomping his way back to the kitchen, he found her standing at the table, making sandwiches. "What is going on?" he snapped when he had joined her.

"Lunch," she quipped, smiling up at him. "Relax, Boo. Blake asked me to look after him. We're going to eat a little lunch. I'll read him a story or something, and tomorrow we will straighten this whole thing out."

"You? You don't even like kids," Rider grumbled. Picking up a slice of bread, he applied some mayo. "Why would Blake ask you?"

Meri glared at him. "I never said I didn't like kids. I said I didn't want any. There's a difference."

"Not much." He added a few slices of lunchmeat and topped it with pickles, then more bread. "Are there any chips?"

"In the pantry." Placing Matthew's sandwich on a plate, she used a knife to cut it in half. "Is this ok, sweetie?"

"Yes," he whispered, accepting the plate from her. A tear spilled over onto his cheek as he lifted it and took a bite.

"See, you already made him cry," Rider pointed out, opening a bag of Lays. "You want some of these?" he offered gruffly.

The boy nodded, wiping at the drop of sadness. Rider sprinkled a few on his plate. "Let's eat in one of the apartments."

"Good idea," Merideth agreed, making her own meal. "But my fridge is empty," she lamented. Opening the one there in the kitchen, she selected a jug of juice and a carton of milk. "These will do."

"Good. All I have is wine and beer." Rider chuckled. "Not very kid friendly."

Carrying his plate with both hands, Matthew walked to

the back of the house between the couple. Arriving at Meri's door, he followed her inside.

"I'll grab a chair from my room," Rider informed them as he placed his sandwich and chips on the table.

His eyes wide, Matt looked around the cramped space. "You have a kitchen in your bedroom," he observed.

Merideth laughed. "Well, I guess I do." Placing the beverages on the table, she fetched glasses from her small set of cabinets. "This is like a little apartment. Do you and your mother live in a house? Or is it an apartment, like this?"

"My momma died," Matthew replied just as Rider returned. Frozen at the boy's words, he slowly lowered the chair to the floor. Turning, he met Merideth's gaze.

"I'm sorry to hear that," she whispered, the tears welling as she blinked to remove them. "I lost my Daddy not too long ago," she added, pouring him some milk, and offering him a chair.

The boy sat, his feet not quite reaching the floor. Swinging them, he crunched a few chips, then asked, "Was your daddy sick? My momma had the 'rona."

Merideth collapsed into her chair. "Your mother had COVID?"

"Yeah. She was sick and I couldn't see her. I stayed with Grandpa Charlie, but she didn't get better. That's why they brought me here. My Father doesn't want me."

His last words were more than Rider could take. "Fuck tomorrow. We are getting to the bottom of this right now." On his feet, he headed to the door.

Merideth caught him in the hall before he could reach the exit into the garden. "Rider, please! Don't ruin Sarah's day."

"There's a little boy in there crying into his sandwich who thinks his Father doesn't want him!" Rider shouted, pointing at the scene through the wall.

"What boy?" Sarah asked, presenting herself from around the corner. Meri and Rider gaped at her, too stunned to speak. The looks of horror on their faces drew her towards them. "What is going on with you two?" It was her wedding day, could they not behave for a few little hours? She stopped at the open portal to her left, glancing inside.

"Sarah, this is not what you think," Merideth began, stepping forward and catching the handle to close the wooden covering.

"Not what I think," Sarah stammered, pushing against it to prevent the latch from catching. Inside Merideth's kitchenette, she scoured the space, taking it all in. "Are you hiding him from me?" She turned to glare at the couple, who had also joined them. "Why would you do that?"

"It's your special day," Matthew provided for them.

"Please, Sarah," Meri regained her composure and took over. "Something has happened, and Blake doesn't want it to spoil your wedding. He asked me to look after him and said we would work it all out tomorrow."

Sarah's face flushed. "I came in for a piss. That's all I wanted." She held up a hand, indicating the boy. "What the fuck is this?"

"He's my son," Blake informed her from the doorway.

"And when were you planning to tell me about this?" she squealed.

"I wasn't," he stated bluntly. He held up the envelope. "His mother hid him from me, and if Madame Demore hadn't seen him during my visit to her about the baby, I would be just as shocked as you are right now." He opened the envelope and read from the first page. "*Dear Judoc. I have done my best to shield our son from the darkness that is your life. However, I am going on the ventilator, and I fear this might be the end for me. If I die, he will be delivered to you. Please care for our son. Matthew means the world to me. Sincerely, Julia.*"

"Who is Julia?" Merideth asked absently.

"She was part of the coven a few years ago." He offered the second page. "She sent his birth certificate, but there's no father's name on it. I guess she expects me to believe that he's mine."

Sarah glared at him, then cut her eyes over to the boy, who had finished his sandwich and was busy crunching the chips. "How can you doubt it?" she whispered. "He looks just like you."

"Yeah. He looks like my brother, too." Blake scowled, stroking his chin. "This doesn't feel right. Especially today." His voice cracked, and he glanced at Sarah in her beautiful dress. "I'm so sorry, pumpkin. I hoped they could keep this quiet and sort it out tomorrow."

"Oh, it's ok, Baby," Sarah soothed, nodding at the mini version of him. Stepping towards her new husband, she pulled him into a hug. "I think the party is about over anyways. I'll go get rid of everyone and we can have a meeting as soon as they are gone."

His arms sliding around her, Blake hugged her tight. "I wanted to celebrate."

"Then let's go celebrate. A little longer," she agreed, sliding out of his grasp and cupping her belly. "Is it Matthew?"

"Yes." He nodded, looking up from his crumbs with enticing blue pools of wonder.

"I like that name." She grinned at him. "I'm going to take your father outside for a bit longer, but I promise, we'll be back inside and figure things out here in a bit."

As soon as the couple had gone, Rider gasped for air.

"Man, she took that well. I just knew it was going to be a tantrum."

Merideth gave him a cold glare. "If you had stayed in here like we were supposed to."

"What? I didn't want to be a party to this, but you dragged me into it," he goaded.

"I'm not going to argue with you." Lifting the boy's suitcase, she held out her hand. "Come on, Matty. Let's go pick out your room," she said confidently, leaving Rider alone to contemplate the error of his ways.

FOURTEEN

Little Secrets

JOSELINE COULD TELL something had changed as soon as Blake and Sarah rejoined the party. Glancing around at the guests, she felt surrounded by their happy thoughts and moods, the couple a strained contrast. "Something's up," she whispered, elbowing her mate.

"Like what?" Karen asked, turning to face her. Sipping from a cup of punch, she smiled.

"Sarah and Blake, that's what," Joseline clipped. "Let's get closer and find out." Grabbing Karen's arm, she steered her across the yard.

"Hi guys!" Karen broke the ice for them. "Everything going ok?"

"Real subtle," Jos rebuked, giving them a smile.

"Well, now that you mention it." Blake grinned at their empath. "We've run into a bit of a snag."

Sarah glanced at him, giggling. "Snag," she mimicked, thinking of the little secret safely tucked inside the house.

"I'm glad you're taking this so well," he said quietly to her.

"So, nothing serious then?" Joseline glanced between them anxiously.

"Nope. We can finish up the celebration," Blake stated firmly. "I need another drink," he added, heading off to find a fresh glass.

As soon as he was gone, Karen planted herself next to Sarah. "Ok, give. What's going on?"

"Blake has a son," Sarah whispered, holding her smile firmly in place. "His mother died, and she had him shipped here."

"Holy shit!" Joseline breathed, glancing nervously around them. "Today?"

"Of course today," Karen whined. "This may be Sarah's birthday, but it has a terrible track record in the long run."

"It will be fine," Sarah rebuked, giving her best friend a sideways glance. "He is an adorable little copy of Blake."

"But he had a child with someone else!" Karen hissed, shaking her dark locks.

"How old is he?" Josee interjected.

"He's not a baby, if that's what you mean." Sarah giggled. "I was probably in high school when he was conceived, so it's not like Blake was cheating on me or anything."

"That's a relief." Karen rolled her eyes, then took a noisy sip of fruity punch. "So, what are we going to do about it?"

"Nothing at the moment. We should enjoy the rest of the event and we'll hold a meeting once all the guests are gone. I need to go say goodbye to my parents," she added. "They are flying back to Atlanta tonight."

"It doesn't creep you out that they came?" Karen sighed. "After you and Blake left their house in the middle of the night, I've been worried what they thought about things. Or what they might do about it."

"I'm beginning to think that worry is a huge waste of time

in most matters," Sarah said stiffly. Lifting her skirt, she picked her way across the grass and presented herself before them. "What did you think?"

"It was a beautiful ceremony," her mother clipped in an odd contrast with her foul expression. Looking her up and down, she added, "You look so happy, sweetheart."

"I am happy, Mom." Sarah grabbed the other woman, hugging her tightly. Pretending to the world that all was normal, she suggested loudly, "Now that travel is back on, I hope to see you a little more often."

Her father laughed. "With the first grandbaby on the way, do you think you can keep her away?" He stared at her, his teeth bared like a wild animal.

Sarah's smile strained, she glanced up at him. Their behavior had always been odd, but with their secret out, she couldn't fathom why they had bothered showing up. "I hope not, Daddy. Both of you are welcome any time." She blinked back tears, wishing their affection had been more than theatrics and show for the other guests. "Next time you'll have to stay longer." She indicated the house. "We have plenty of room."

"Oh, our hotel will suffice," her mother informed her, pushing her away. "We don't want to impose." Their words sounded contrived, as if they were reciting lines to a bad play.

"We'll consider it the next visit," her father added, seeing her contorted features. "I know you wanna keep us close," he drawled.

Her chin dimpled, Sarah whispered, "Thanks, Daddy." She wondered if the opposite were true, and she and the baby would be the ones being kept close.

"Oh, look at the time!" Tanya exclaimed, glancing at her phone. "We'll miss our flight if we're not careful."

"We'll be fine." Tim pulled his assumed daughter into a hug. "You take care of yourself, pumpkin."

"I will, Daddy," she uttered, closing her eyes, wishing she understood what to make of them.

Blake joined her as Tim and Tanya took the side path around the house. "Are you ok, love?" he asked quietly.

"I suppose that I am." She sighed deeply.

"To be honest, I was shocked as shit when they showed up here," he confessed.

"I know. Rider told me." She cut her eyes over at him with a grin.

He snorted, then took a gulp from his glass. "And they didn't say a word about our visit a few weeks ago."

"Nope. Almost like they forgot all about it." She glanced around at the thinning crowd. "Some have already gone, I think."

"The sun is getting low in the sky," Blake observed. "I guess it's time to run everyone off. It is Halloween, after all, and everyone has their party plans for the evening to get to."

"Yeah. A big night," she agreed. They had said their vows, thrown the bouquet, and cut the cake, so the major milestones had been covered. She glanced at the table of gifts. "I'll have the girls take those inside. We'll open them later and send out thank you cards."

The yard empty a short time later, they gathered bags of trash in case it rained, but everything else they left for the morning. Back inside, they found that Merideth has already put Matthew into the first bedroom on the left, at the top of the stairs. They had unpacked his suitcase, and all his things were safely stored in his drawers. Lying in the bed asleep, he took their breaths away when they peeked in to see him.

"So, how does he fit into things?" Joseline asked, indicating the Blake's mini-me with an open palm.

"Let's go downstairs," Meri suggested, closing the door.

"You should have chosen another room. Right at the top of the stairs, he'll hear everything," Rider pointed out.

"He chose the room," Merideth clipped, raising her chin defiantly.

"But he's really Blake's son?" Karen asked.

"The letter says that he is." Sarah held it up, having read it several times, as if searching for clues between the lines. She had changed into a simple pair of pajamas and curled into her end of the couch to tuck her sock feet beneath her.

"Then it's settled," Joseline confirmed with a nod, noting how spent the bride really was.

Blake pinched the bridge of his nose, closing his eyes for a moment. "Not exactly. I'm not going to accept this until we get one of those DNA tests."

"But you slept with her, right?" Rider pointed out, still disturbed by their actions towards the boy.

"Yes, but I'm sure my brother did as well. Most of the girls in the coven were…community property." Blake shook his head to clear it. "Besides the fact that I am extremely careful with my seed. I have been very diligent, as I told Madam Demore. I don't give it to just anyone." He glanced at Sarah. "There is no way he can be my kid."

"But I saw it," Merideth said quietly.

"You saw what?" Blake asked, his voice dropping a level.

"I don't know how to describe it," she whined. "When I touched him, I saw the girl. His mother, Julia. She was terrified when she realized you had gotten her pregnant. She was certain you were the father, and she immediately abandoned her life here. She fled to Michigan, of all places, to hide from you."

"I think she was from there," Blake said even more quietly, his heart thumping in his chest. He nodded, considering her words, then recalling how highly he had praised her talents only a few weeks before. "I still want a test," he insisted.

"Do you want an official one, or will the DNA family history thing do?" Joseline asked. "I'm sure we can get the ancestry one done pretty easily."

"I want a real one. If I'm going to be responsible for him, we have to be sure." Blake stormed out of the room and into the kitchen hoping none of them would follow him.

FIFTEEN

Terms of Surrender

A WEEK LATER, Merideth sat at the kitchen table with Rider and Matthew, each with a square of paper before them. Water and a pallet of paints occupied the center of the table. "Are you comfortable?" she asked, glancing at the stack of books they had used as a booster.

"I'm fine," the boy replied. Dobbing at his page, he grinned. "I made green." He smiled up at Rider, pointing at his creation.

"You sure did." Seated next to him, the man could not have been more pleased. Calmly rinsing his brush, he flicked his eyes over to her. "How was your date?"

Merideth glared at him, waiting for the jab. When it didn't come, her features softened. "It was fine."

"Does he have a job?"

She had gone out with him for the third time only a few nights before. When she brought him in to introduce him to the group, Rider had avoided meeting the man filling his shoes. "Of course." She swallowed. "He's an accountant."

"Oh, that's nice. He'll be great for Inside and Out," he observed. Dropping his arm behind Matty's shoulders, he instructed, "Squish the water out a little more, hon. That way your paper won't get so soggy."

"Like this?" he asked, searching for approval.

"Yes, much better," Rider praised. Glancing back at her, he added, "Does he have any hobbies?"

Adding paint to her brush, Meri flushed. "I'm not sure we should talk about this," she said.

"Not a problem. I think Karen is going to fix me up with a friend from school," he added. Chuckling, he sat up straight and stretched. "I don't think it's going to work out."

Her face shot up and she glared at him. "You're not even going to give her a chance?"

"Oh, I'll go out with her. Once or twice should make Karen happy."

"But…" Meri prodded. "If you haven't even met her, how can you judge?"

"She's probably a decade behind me," he pointed out. "Besides, as a witch, I'll outlive any mortal by a lifetime or two." He shrugged, glancing at the boy. "It doesn't feel right," he concluded. "Does your accountant seem as if he knows anything of the craft?"

Shaking her head, Meri sighed. "I hadn't really thought about it. I guess I could ask Blake. See if he can sniff him out for me and give me the verdict."

"That's a good idea." Rider pointed at her. "I'll be sure to introduce Cheryl up front. Get that out of the way before I make any judgements."

Merideth continued to dob her paint, covertly watching Rider give Matty lessons. Open and free with him, the pair obviously enjoyed the process. As the minutes ticked by, a cloud settled over her. The painting she had started may have been bright and happy, but it quickly took on a dark appearance as her emotions trickled onto the page.

"Meri's making rain," Matt pointed out, smiling at her. "Are we getting lunch soon?"

"I'll make us sandwiches when we're finished painting," she promised.

"Ok." He bounced his feet against his chair. "I want chips, too."

"There always has to be chips," Rider agreed, tussling his black locks.

They seemed so comfortable together. The man across from her would make an excellent father someday. Her thoughts drifted, and she recalled the dinner conversation the night she met the accountant. *"I don't want to get married, and I have no plans for children,"* she had informed him decisively. A bit heavy for a first date.

"Who does?" he had replied tartly. *"Not in this day and age."*

"Albert," she said aloud, then added, "that's his name. The accountant."

"Ok." Rider nodded, not looking up at her.

"He plays golf," she continued.

"Lovely. Will he teach you to play?"

"I didn't ask. We talked a great deal about the business," she confessed. Actually, Albert had become quite enthralled by the subject as soon as she had mentioned it. Her mind retracing the conversations she had shared with him, she realized they had spoken of little else. "How's your studio coming along?"

Rider smiled at her. "It's going to be great. But one doesn't really open an art studio for the money," he explained.

"I didn't say that they did," she whispered, blinking away her tears. She leaned back in her chair, watching the pair for another minute, then she got to her feet. "I'm going to start on those sandwiches. Maybe we can sneak them in while we work."

Putting Matty's together, she cut it in two. Adding chips to the side, she poured half a glass of milk, then placed them beside him. Her hand absently rested on his head as she admired his work. "Is that an abstract?"

"It's a house." Blake's offspring pointed out a few of the features. "This is the roof, and this is a big tree."

"Is there a swing in it?" Rider asked, peeking over to see.

"I'm going to make one," Matty agreed. "After my sandwich," he added, lifting a square and chomping it.

Turning to the counter, Meri thought she would make her own sandwich, but instead she piled on meat and mayo, then topped it with pickles. As she added the second slice of bread, she stared at it, recalling all the meals she had handed to Rider while his head was stuck in a painting. Too many to count. Adding chips to his plate as well, she sat it beside him.

"Oh, thank you, Boo," Rider offered without a second thought.

"You're welcome, Boo." She caught her hand before it stroked the back of his head and neck. Curling the fingers, she leaned against the counter to watch the pair. Covering her mouth with the hand, she pressed her lips together behind it, the realization of all that she had given up welling inside her.

"Are you not eating?" Rider asked, his sandwich already half gone.

"I am. I just need to put it together." She turned her back on them, slowly building her lunch. Her fingers shook, and she stared at them, her focus drawn to that special one. She could hear Albert's words ringing in the back of her mind. *"Who does? Not in this day and age."*

"I do," she whispered, the realization slamming into her

like a freight train, sending her heart pounding. "I'll be right back," she called as she left them, scurrying to her sanctuary.

Closing the door, she leaned her back against it. Covering her face with her hands, she didn't know whether to laugh or to cry. "But what is Rider going to say?" Thinking about it made her stomach queasy. "He might be more interested in a new start with Cheryl," she pointed out.

Crossing the room, she opened the single drawer in her nightstand to peer down at the plain white box. "No, you don't," she told herself firmly, closing it with a slam. Turning, she sat on the bed and stared at the drawer.

She heard muffled laughter tinkle in through the closed door. "Yes, you do." She quickly opened it once more, snatching up the box and prying the lid. Her hands shook, the metal cold against her skin. Sliding the ring out, she examined it. "So perfect," she whispered. She hadn't realized how well Rider knew her. And she him.

Sliding the band onto her finger, she admired the curl of diamonds. "It's just a signal. I'm not agreeing to anything. I only want to talk." On her feet, she marched back to the kitchen and finished making her lunch. Placing her plate on the table with a flourish, she ate hungrily, noting Rider and Matty had finished theirs.

"I think we have some cake," Rider recalled. "Do we need a slice of that?" he offered.

"I like ice cream," Matthew informed him, his masterpiece almost complete. "See my swing, Meri?"

"I do!" She grinned anxiously at him, not daring to look at Rider.

"Ice cream it is," the man huffed, getting out of his chair, and setting out the bowls. "Would you like a scoop, Boo?"

"I'd love some," she choked, feeling faint.

When he placed hers before her, he pointed at her hand,

not wanting to corner her. "What is that, exactly?" he asked, giving her the chance to define it.

She glanced at the sparkle, then cut her eyes up at him. "A truce. If you'll have one."

Elation swept over him, making it hard to reclaim his chair. "I could talk terms," he agreed, as he forced his rear into it. Taking a bite of the creamy sweetness, he beamed.

"You're not playing this hand very tightly," she observed, folding her napkin, and then picking up her bowl. "I can see your cards."

"They're all on the table," he replied.

Matty looked across the flat surface, then under it to the floor. "I don't see any cards."

The couple laughed, and she flicked the ring. "I can't believe it fits."

"You never tried it on?" he asked in surprise.

"Nope. I hadn't given it a second thought, until today." She glanced at the little man next to him. "I'm not promising anything has changed," she added softly. "I still need to be in control of my future."

"Just take me with you," he pleaded. "I sure don't want to be left behind."

"Oh, am I missing lunch?" Ezamay asked, her timing perfect.

"And desert," Matthew quipped, licking his spoon.

"I'll get there," the older woman informed him with a pat on the head. Her eyes missing nothing, she gasped, turning her back to hide her shocked expression. "I guess you two are enjoying your day off," she observed, rather than admit what she'd seen.

"We are," Rider agreed casually. "But I think we are going for a walk in the garden, if you don't mind taking over." Rising, he waited at the door, hoping she would join him.

Her bowl empty, Meri stood slowly, placing it in the sink. "We'll be outside if you need us," she offered, kissing her mother on the cheek.

"Take your time. We're going to go have a story and a nap," the old woman purred, giving the ring a quick glance.

"Would it upset you?" Meri whispered.

"Not at all, honey." Reaching, Ezamay pulled her into a hug. "Do what makes you happy, child. Life's too short for anything less."

"Even witch lives?" Rider asked, obviously hearing them.

"Especially witch lives," Meri agreed, dabbing at a tear as she turned to join him. "Ok, let's go talk about the terms of your surrender."

SIXTEEN

A Wolf Among Us

"Wow, the house is quiet," Sarah observed as she and Blake entered via the front door.

"We're in here," Ezamay called to the couple. At the table when they entered the kitchen, she and Matthew were placing toppings on a home-made pizza. "You're just in time," she informed them with a sly smile.

Sarah opened the fridge to retrieve her juice. Taking a chair, she removed her shoes to rub her feet. "I think I'm standing too much. My dogs are barking something fierce."

"I don't hear any dogs," Matthew pointed out. "Are they puppies?"

"No, she's talking about her feet, sugar," Ezamay said with a giggle.

Holding the bridge of his nose, Blake tried not to laugh. "Oh, son," he whispered. Lifting his face, he gave his bride a smile. "Do you need anything, sweetness?"

"Which is better, hot or cold?" she asked. Seeing his face scrunch, she added. "For sore feet."

"Are they swollen?" Ezamay asked, frightened it could be a bad sign.

"Not really. I just get tired. I was thinking of a soak," Sarah replied, continuing to rub at them.

"I'll make a warm bowl for you," Blake suggested, fishing a large pan out of the pantry. "You want to sit in here, or on the couch?"

"In here, I think. I can smell that pizza already," she teased.

"We just put it in," Ezamay clarified. "Go sit on the couch for a few minutes and take a rest."

On the sofa as instructed, Sarah dipped her toes to test, then plunged her feet in. "Oh, that feels so good."

Sitting across from her on the coffee table, Blake was applying the fluffy towel to them when Rider and Meri came out of their hallway together. All smiles, the couple disappeared into the kitchen without so much as a glance their way.

"Did we just miss something," Sarah breathed, looking up at her mate.

"I don't know, but I'm sure going to find out." Polishing her quickly, he dropped the rag on the couch and lifted the bowl, then marched after them.

Pushing herself up, and a bit slower, Sarah hobbled along behind. "Hey, guys," she said loudly. "It looks like you had a good day off." Plunking back into her seat, she sipped her juice and waited, the couple seated across from her enjoying glasses of wine.

Meri's face a soft pink, she smiled. "Yes, it was a very pleasant day." Taking a drink of her wine, the light danced off her ring.

"So, was that the makeup sex?" Blake asked bluntly, leaning against the counter to enjoy the show.

Her hair swept up into a loose bun, Meri's entire neck and

face took on a deeper shade of red. Casually, Rider ran his finger along the back of her bare hairline, then said, "No corners." He cut his eyes over at his friend, his look speaking volumes.

"They had a goo-ood nap." Matty informed them. "They slept longer than Grammy and me did."

Stunned, Blake gaped at them, unsure which to pounce on first. Deciding to tackle both, he grunted. "I'm sure it was a great *nap*. Grammy? That's new."

"We've picked out my grandma name," Ezamay replied crisply. Wiping down the table, she set plates out. "Blake, can you pull the pizza for us?"

"Sure," he agreed, giving Merideth a crooked grin.

"Please don't tease me, Blake," she begged as he placed a slice on her plate.

"I'm not going to," he promised, taking his seat after they had all been served. "Rider on the other hand –"

"You can't get a rise out of me. It's been too perfect of a day," Rider informed him confidently.

"Awe come on, maybe a little? I mean after the whole pantry thing, I think you deserve a little ribbing," Blake pointed out smugly.

"Ok. Maybe a little." The other man laughed loudly, then raised his glass to Merideth. "I'm sorry, Boo. Our magister isn't going to let it go, so just ignore him."

"No, seriously," Sarah interrupted. "Are you guys making it official?" She glanced at the diamond band.

"It was a nice nap," Meri quipped with a shrug. Cutting her eyes over at Rider, she rolled her tongue. "I missed you, Boo."

"I missed you, too." He leaned towards her, planting a simple kiss on her lips.

Exchanging a glance, Sarah shook her head at Blake. "Don't tease them," she suggested. "In front of your son," she added with a loud giggle.

"Aww, thanks." Merideth laughed as well. "Ok, fine. We haven't decided anything yet. But we can both admit, we are miserable when we aren't together. I'm going to wear the ring for a while, and we'll see how it goes."

"So, it's more like a promise ring," Blake suggested, finishing off his slice.

"Yeah, I guess you could call it that," Rider agreed amicably. "How about you guys? Did everything run smoothly at the store?"

"Yeah, where's the girls?" Ezamay asked, missing her other daughter.

"They have a double date with Hannah and Hubert," Sarah said quietly, glancing at Matty, then cutting the gaze over to Blake.

"I still don't like him. I've tried, but he just doesn't sit with me the right way," he confessed.

"I should take Matt up for his bath," May suggested. "That way you four can talk."

Blake stared at his son, realizing what she meant. "That's probably a good idea. Thanks, Grammy," he added as she guided the young man out.

Once they had heard the duo climb the stairs, Sarah blurted, "Ok, what's wrong with Hubert? It has to be something. I don't' think you would hold this kind of grudge on a hunch."

Blake met the other man's eyes, considering how much he should reveal. "Let's just say, we have proof that he's visited my brother. Probably more than once."

"Oh, no!" Merideth gasped, leaning towards the table to keep her voice low. "Does Joseline know about this?"

"We don't know," Rider provided. "We've kept it quiet, hoping we would learn more, but so far Sis seems oblivious to her brother's actions."

Merideth grimaced. "Well surely there is a way we can test her."

"If there is, I don't know about it. Unless you have some seer trick you can use on her," Blake suggested.

"Are you sure your proof is solid?" Sarah asked, still not convinced.

"I paid a guard to watch. He texted me just before we returned from Virginia that Bert had been to the prison. We have a wolf among us," Blake informed her flatly.

"And if Joseline is still tied to Morcant, it could be two," Rider added solemnly.

"No, Joseline wouldn't do that," Meri insisted. "She's solid with the coven. I'm sure of it."

"Do you have a way to test her?" Blake asked, leaning on his elbows to fold his hands in front of his face, tapping them against his lips. "We need to be sure."

"I'll see if I can devise a way," Meri whispered, guilt forming in the pit of her gut. "But she's my sister. It may be difficult."

"Do your best," Blake suggested, returning to his glass. "I'm all out. Anyone want to open a new bottle?"

"I can't," Sarah reminded him.

"And we're going to bed soon." Rider declined politely, giving Merideth a grin.

"Oh!" Sarah gasped. "If you two are getting back together, Ezamay can use your room." Her face immediately flushed, as if she'd been caught at something sinister.

Rider cocked his head. "I'm not sure we are going to move back in together just yet. We didn't actually discuss it today." He looked at Meri, wanting her say.

"That's fine with me." She shrugged. "You could take all your work to the new gallery. Maybe keep a bit here for the evenings."

"I think you are missing the point here, guys. Why does Ezamay need a new room?" Blake asked, eyeing the others warily.

Meri lowered her gaze guiltily. "My mother has decided to sell her place. She says there are too many memories with Daddy there." Looking up, she grimaced. "I'm sure it would only be temporary. She'll probably get an apartment or buy a house here."

Looking at Sarah, Blake rubbed his chin. "How'd you know about this?"

"I overheard her talking to a realtor," the red-head confessed. "She made me promise not to tell anyone about the move. She and I agreed to make her our nanny once Matty's test is back and it's all official. Then we were going to decide where she would stay permanently." Glancing between the couple across from her she breathed a sigh of relief. "I didn't realize she had told you. Thank God I didn't spill it."

"Grammy." Rider chuckled. "I guess she figures that'll be as close to grandmother as she'll ever get."

"And I'm fine with that," she informed them loudly from the door.

"Oh, Mother." Merideth gasped, sitting up straight. "I thought you were giving Matthew his bath."

"I was." The older woman reclaimed her chair. "Now he's in bed, waiting for his story."

"I'll do it," Sarah sang, moving gently on her tired feet. "I love story time!" she called as she left the room.

"Just when I think we are getting things worked out, something else crops up," Blake lamented. Tapping the side of his empty glass, he looked around at the three of his remaining coven members. "You know I'm going to need the three of you, right?"

Catching her breath, Meri stared at him. "For what?"

Ezamay nodded. "We here, Judoc. Let him come. We'll be ready."

SEVENTEEN

Back to Business

AFTER WORK A FEW EVENINGS LATER, Sarah collected their mail as usual. Flipping through it, she paused at the return address on one of the pieces. "Oh my God, it came," she whispered, fully aware of what the envelope contained.

Climbing the stairs slowly, she arrived at their bedroom door with her heart in her throat. She closed the portal behind her as she entered to ensure their privacy. The letter in her hand, it trembled as she offered it to her mate. "This came today."

"Already?" Blake stared at it. "We just had the blood drawn a few days ago. I thought the post office was broken and it would take weeks to get the results." He laughed anxiously, still not moving to accept it from her.

Wafting it towards him, she whispered, "I can't open it. You're his father, it's yours to see first."

Snatching it away from her, Blake ripped off the end and slid the paper out. He stared at the page, his mind numb.

"What did they find?" she asked, trying to get a look at it over his arm.

He crumpled the paper. "It says I am not his father. My

brother is." A tear formed and his eye, and he dabbed at it angrily. Fighting with his emotions, the pressure of it had all but broken him, and now: this. "Damn it. For months I have had this weighing on me. Pressing on me in the back of my mind. Believing that I had sired a child with some worthless wench, who ran away. And now that he's here and we've had time to know him..." His voice cracked, and he paused to recover. "Now, I discover he really isn't mine." He looked up at her. "I'm so angry that all of this...so heartbroken that this has happened. I'm sorry, love. I know this hasn't been easy for you."

"But darling," Sarah whispered, clinging to his stiff form. "He could still be yours. Madam Demore said –"

"Fuck what she said. She was wrong. Again." He cut her off cleanly. Pursing his lips, he pressed the back of his hand against them as he followed that line of thought. "Unless I don't tell anyone the results. If I lie, then he would be my son." He bobbled his head side to side, processing that scenario. "And she would have been right." Still on the verge of tears, he glared at her. "Is that what you want?"

"Well, I do feel so connected to him," she soothed. "His name is Matthew." Blake held the scowl, so she added, "My maiden name was Matthews." She smiled encouragingly, almost able to see the conflict roiling within him.

"Bah, that's just a coincidence," he muttered, pulling away from her to pace the room. Safely on the other side, he turned to face her, waving the results. "What possible good could come from claiming my brother's son?"

"What will happen to him if you don't?" Strain distorted her features. "Morcant is in prison, love. Where would Matt go? Who would care for him with his mother gone?" She straightened, strengthening her resolve. "Even if we kept him while Morcant is away, what darkness would he be exposed to once your brother is free and can take possession of him?"

"Well, this isn't exactly a well of light around here," Blake groused, waving his arms to indicate their wayward coven.

"Any evil here is your brother's doing. We do our best to fight against it." She recalled their visit to Loren and the words she had given them in Savannah. "I think Matthew is the child you both hold at stake," she observed firmly.

"Ah, no. Don't use that witch's words against me," he snapped. "We still haven't deciphered their full meaning."

"Exactly." Sarah sighed, shaking her head. "I don't think we can afford to send him away. To break his little heart only again. The price would be too great, especially for him. Admit that you love him."

"How I feel isn't really the point." He rocked his jaw, his stance softening. "Is this really what you want. Me to claim someone else's bastard child."

"You are the only one who can," she said quietly. "His own mother believed you were his father. You could make it so with the utterance of a word. And to hell with what the test says."

Blake turned away, running his palm over his lips and chin roughly as he considered her plan. "He does show a reverence to me. He is also convinced, which is likely his mother's doing. He has brought no trouble, other than arranging for his care, and between the group of us, that's not an issue, now is it." He faced her abruptly. "He can't hang around at the shop all day, following us around. He needs lessons. School. And a caregiver." He paused, making the connection. "Ezamay."

"Exactly as we planned." She smiled at him, her fingers tracing the line of her belly. "We can enroll him in school, and she will be here to meet him in the afternoons. Of course, he should be allowed to visit the shop on the weekends. He loves it there."

Blake considered her words, watching her hands move across her bump, then indicated it with a nod. "It's a girl, isn't it? You're afraid I will be denied a son after all."

She laughed at him. "I haven't asked, so I really don't know. But they could grow up together as siblings, either way." She stepped towards him, her green eyes bright. "Please say yes. Give him this chance at a better life."

Blake stared at her. "This is crazy. How is this for a stepmother to behave? Aren't you supposed to be evil and harsh, providing nothing but suffering and pain?" he mocked.

She shook her head. "I can admit it. I adore that little man." Her lip quivered, but she stopped herself from stooping to pure begging, at least at that point.

He turned his gaze to the page. Seizing the trashcan, he lit it on fire and dropped it into the canister, watching until it had disintegrated into a smudge of ash at the bottom. "No one must ever know. You promise me you will take this secret to your grave."

"Of course. He is our son, and we will do all that we can to protect him. Them. Equally." She massaged herself again, and Blake dropped the canister to the floor, then placed a large hand on the curve of her belly.

"Ok. Then tomorrow morning we'll share the news before we take him to the school." Caressing her, he hoped she was right, and that they were doing to the right thing. But at the same time, waiting until morning gave him a full night to change his mind.

"We got the results!" Blake announced loudly as the trio entered the shop the following morning. "Everyone gather around." He wiggled his fingers above his head, indicating for them to form a group. His eyes sweeping the ring of friendly faces, he drew a deep breath and smiled. "What a roller coaster these last few weeks have been, right?"

The group laughed, and Meri smiled broadly. Dropping her arm across Matty's shoulders, she hugged him slightly. "Don't be nervous," she whispered. "You and I will be friends, either way."

"I can formally announce that today, I have a son." Blake held up his flattened hand, indicating the boy in question. "And that means we will be enrolling him in school this very morning. And completing all the necessary paperwork to have his name changed as soon as humanly possible."

The group cheered, and Hannah beamed. "Does that mean I'm losing my little helper already?" He'd only been to the shop a few days, but her heart had been stolen on the first.

"I'm afraid so." Blake shrugged. "He'll be here on the weekends, though, I'm sure." He smiled down at his boy, who had stepped out of Merideth's grasp to stand before him. "You will have Grammy to stay with in the afternoons, and magic will fill your life if you wish it." He knelt before him, noticing the boy's sedate features. "You don't seem pleased, though. Does this not make you happy?"

"It does, Father." Matthew nodded, slipping into Blake's strong arms for a hug.

Enclosing him tightly, Blake placed his hand on the back of the small head, inhaling the scent of him. "I'm sorry about your mother," he whispered. "I cannot bring her back. And I cannot replace the years she took from us by hiding you from me." He lessened his grip, allowing the child to stand firm and met his gaze. "I will do my best to make our lives whole from here," he promised.

This time, Matt smiled, his missing teeth exposed. "I know you will, Father."

Blake tousled his hair. "Father sounds so stiff, my boy. I'm hoping some day I might qualify as Dad."

Rider cringed at his use of the word. "There's nothing special about either term," he growled, ready to retreat to his studies in the basement.

Blake shook his head, refusing to be baited. "So, it's business as usual from here on. Let's get the store recovered and restocked." He rubbed his hands together quickly, then laughed. "And make some money today."

EIGHTEEN

In the Shadows

STANDING IN HIS BATHROOM, Hubert combed his hair, smelled his breath, then sniffed his pits. All passing inspection, he flexed his muscles and examined them under the bright lights in the mirror over the sink. Only wearing his boxers, he hoped he appeared sexy to the girl in the next room.

Taking her time to get ready for bed, Hannah turned down the blankets and cut off the overhead light. Putting on a single lamp, she grinned at the dim, shadowiness of the room. "Perfect."

She and Bert had slept together a few times, but tonight would be different. Over dinner, they had talked of moving in together, and therefore, this signified the beginning of their new lives together. "Honey," she called into the adjacent master bath. "Are you coming soon?"

"Yeah, give me another sec," he hollered back, gripping the sink before him. A strange twinge had caught him in the chest and made it hard to breathe. Doubling over, he could feel his hands go numb. Rubbing his digits against the cool marble top, he gasped. "What the hell?" He couldn't feel a thing.

A moment later, the lack of sensation spread to his knees and his legs buckled. On the floor, he panicked, afraid he was having a heart attack or something. Closing his eyes, he fought for his breath. When the lids fluttered open, he no longer operated them.

His body stood, shaking head to toe, but Bert had no control over the motion. *What the fuck is this?* he thought to himself. "Hey, sexy." He heard his voice. *I did not say that!*

Leaning over to fluff the pillows, Hannah swished her rear for him as her butt cheeks peeked out from under her nighty.

Sauntering into the room, Bert toyed with her arm, sliding his fingers gently down it. Lifting her digits, he kissed them. "What do you say we try something new tonight?"

"Like what?" she breathed, intoxicated by his smile.

"Oh, you know. Everyone is trying out the whole S and M thing." He could see the shock in her sea green orbs. "Nothing too wild, mind you." He cocked his hips, rocking them a bit. "Just a little spice, if you know what I mean." He waited, seeing her consider it.

"Oh, you're gonna love it," he finished, pulling her by the hand and helping position her on the bed. "You lie down right there. I'm going to gather a few things for us," he insisted, leaving her to get comfortable on the pliable surface. Opening the closet door, he noticed the rack of neckties. "Perfect."

No, they're not perfect! Bert screamed inside his own head, but the girl could not hear, and his body refused to obey. His thoughts running in circles, he suddenly had an idea. *Morcant!* Confident he had discovered the cause, he focused. *Morcant, stop this! I forbid you to touch her.* But at the same time, he recalled permission had already been given. Morcant intended to initiate her into the coven, and he had agreed.

By that time, Morcant had her tied, her arms firmly bound to the headboard on either side. "See if you can escape," he prodded.

Pulling against the bonds, she squirmed, noting they only got tighter when she tried. "Nope." Looking up at Bert's face, she sighed. "Don't I get a safe word or something? You know, in case things get out of hand."

Morcant stood up straight, glaring down at her. "Well, I guess you can have one. If you don't trust me." He added a small pout.

"Oh, I trust you." The girl smiled up at him, nodding. "It's ok, baby. I don't really need one."

NO! No, baby. Get the safe word, Bert begged, realized at the same time it wouldn't matter to Morcant if she used it.

Turning to the nightstand, Morcant rummaged through the drawers. Finding an old tube of lube, he pulled it out and tested the freshness.

"What's that?" Hannah asked innocently, lifting her head to see better.

"Oh, it's just in case we decide to try some anal."

Anal! No way had he ever dared suggest such a thing. *She's got to know this isn't me!* He whined inside his prison.

But as things moved on, Bert realized that she didn't know. Completely clueless, she allowed Morcant more and more latitude. When prompted, she lifted her rear for him, giggling as he slid her frilly panties down her silky legs. He rubbed her up and down, sliding his hands along her inner thighs. "Are you nasty, Hannah?" his voice asked.

She smiled at him. "I don't know. Would you like me to be?" She cocked a leg for him, and Bert watched his fingers dart inside her, toying with her wetness before he licked them.

"Mmm, that's good," his voice claimed, although he tasted nothing. *Hannah, please don't let this happen.*

Morcant lifted her pretty negligee, sucking and biting her beautiful breasts. Tied as she was, she squealed, suggesting it was painful, but she had no way to stop him. "That's a little rough, darling," she prodded, her voice under control.

"Just relax, sweet pea," Morcant cooed. Laying over her, he rubbed her forcefully, then caught a fist full of hair. He ground his teeth as he pulled it tighter, not stopping until she screeched. "You love me, don't you Hannah?" he growled.

"You know I do," she whimpered, tears welling in her clear green orbs. Their eyes locked, she could feel his cock slip inside her pussy, his grasp on her hair holding her head in the awkward position.

"Damn, you are sopping," he moaned, pumping against her.

"You forgot your condom," she stammered.

"We don't need it tonight." He groaned, hoisting her legs, then pausing. "Help me out a little here, love."

Glaring at him, Hannah chewed her lip. Her thoughts racing, she considered her options.

"Come on baby," Morcant purred, releasing her mane. "I love you so much. Play with me a little."

Slowly, reluctantly, she raised her legs, parting them and granting him full access.

Laying over her, Bert sobbed inside himself, unable to stop what was happening. Unable to end his view of the horror. At least he couldn't feel any of it, but that held little consolation as he watched it unfold.

He cringed at the horrible look of shock on her face when Morcant shoved his finger in her ass. She pulled at her bindings and would certainly have pushed it away if she had been able.

He sobbed inwardly at cries and whimpers that had no effect on the man controlling his body. Her eyes parted wide at some other action he couldn't ascertain, but Morcant pushed harder, fighting for more.

"Honey!" she squawked. "I don't think I want to do that!"

"Oh, relax," Morcant chided. "You're gonna love it, I swear. Here, I'll get some lube." He sat up, adding a bit to his fingers, then reinserted his cock into her pussy. Holding her legs up with his shoulders, his finger found the pucker and pushed its way inside. "See? Nice and easy." He stopped pumping his hips, only using the digit to fuck her ass, then he bent over, kissing her. Bending further, he returned to her bruised nipples. "Damn, you are so hot."

Pulling against the straps on her wrists, they tightened. "My hands hurt," she complained.

"Here, let me help." Morcant grabbed a spare tie. Rolling it, he shoved it in her mouth. When she fought against it, he slapped her. Then he applied the back of his hand to the other side. "Be still," he commanded. "I don't want to hurt you, but I will."

Shocked at his angry words, Hannah lay there, blinking up at him through the strands of golden hair that landed across her face. Catching her legs, Morcant folded her, exposing the pucker he prized most. Using two fingers this time, he massaged it, coating it with the gooey gel. "I won't go all the way, I promise."

Dipping his cock in her wet pussy, he gave her a few strokes, then pushed her up. Lining up on his new target, he slowly let her down against it.

"Uh, uhhh," she squealed, her tongue working against the gag. A tear escaped, sliding down into her hair.

Grabbing a pillow, Morcant covered her face. Then he squeezed her calves, using them to rock her hips to each side, wiggling her to massage his way in. With the tip in placed, he folded her again. He pressed down on her legs, his cock hard as he pumped slow and evenly, taking a little more of her with each stroke. "You can't fight it," he instructed. "Just let it go."

Releasing a leg, he pulled the pillow out of the way. Her face frozen, she gasped for air through her nose. Catching the tie, he unwound it from her mouth. "Hannah? I'm in," he panted. "Just relax. It feels so good." He squeezed his hips, his motion smoother as he fucked her. "I'm gonna cum, baby. I'm gonna squirt your ass full of juices."

"Please hurry," she whispered, closing her eyes and rocking her head on the pillow. "It hurts so bad."

"I know. Just a little more." He pushed deeper, and she tightened. "Don't go tense!" He stopped moving. "You have to relax." When the vice around his cock had loosened, he moved again, slower this time. "That's it, baby. You're doing it. You'll be a porn star before you know it!"

Quickening his pace, he pushed for a little more, almost filling her. "Damn, you feel so good. I love you, baby," he groaned, shooting his load, then draping himself over her.

Laying across her, Bert regained control a few minutes later. Pushing himself up, he stared down at her clear green eyes. "Are you ok?" he whispered.

"Yeah. I'm fine. Can you untie me now?"

"Sure, sweetheart!" He panted, loosening each of the hands, his gut wrenching at the cuts and groves in her wrists.

"Are they bad?" She whimpered, rubbing at the raw flesh as she inspected them.

"They'll be ok," he soothed. Noticing blood where her ass met the mattress, he cringed, horrified Morcant could control him at will. "Let's get in the shower," he suggested, wondering if he should tell her what had really happened and terrified what he could do if Morcant did it again.

NINETEEN

The Choices We Make

BERT DROVE Hannah to the store the following morning. She hardly spoke to him, much less looked at him. Reaching across the console, he offered her his hand.

Reluctantly, she slid her fingers between his. "I'm ok with last night," she informed him quietly. "I didn't realize you were into that sort of thing. That's all."

"Baby, if you're not sure, I'm ok with not doing it," he countered, hoping Morcant would leave her alone after having her. "I'm sorry I surprised you with it. We should have talked first."

"It's ok." She squeezed his digits. "Heat of the moment." She cocked her head, looking at him, and her blonde waves cascaded down the side of her face.

"Yeah," he agreed. Pulling up in front of the store, he indicated the parking lot dotted with cars. "Looks like you already have customers."

"Yes. Blake is opening us an hour earlier now. On account of the coffee bar." She grinned, looking around. "Business is good." She had worn her makeup thick that morning and considered putting on her shades. "Do I look ok?" she asked hesitantly.

You look great, baby!" He grinned at her, feeling like a heel for not explaining.

Inside, Blake held down the register. Taking payments and making change, he soaked up the praises for their latest installation. As soon as they entered, his features darkened. He had caught a whiff of the craft on Hubert several times. It was part of the reason he didn't like him. But today, he reeked of it. "Hi guys," he managed, noticing Hannah and the extra thick icing around her eyes. "Hard night?"

"A bit rough," she agreed, stashing her purse beneath the counter.

"Ah. Young lovers," Blake quipped, cutting Hubert an angry glare.

Catching his gaze, the other man swallowed. "Hey, Blake."

"Hi, Bert. Would you have a minute? I've got something I need to discuss with you." Blake made the invitation smoothly, no inkling of what lay in store.

"Sure. Should I wait in your office?" Hubert grinned, hoping he appeared calm.

"Great. The coffee pot is downstairs if you want to wait in the break room," the shop owner offered.

"Thanks." Bert nodded, then disappeared.

Having sensed Hannah's conflicted feelings, Joseline joined them. "How are things today?" she asked, leaning towards the girl.

"I'm fine," Hannah snapped, a bit too quickly. Smiling, she adjusted her hair to cover the bruises on the side of her face, exposing the rope burns on her wrists.

"You don't look fine," Blake growled. Catching her arm, he pushed up her sleeve. "What the hell is this?"

"I told you. Rough night." She gave him her best smile. "Some of us like it that way."

"I bet." Blake pivoted, leaving her and heading down the stairs. Arriving in the near empty break area, he demanded, "What's your side to this story?"

Looking up at him, Hubert faltered. "What story?"

"She looks pretty banged up. I don't see a scratch on you. Did you tie her up before you did that to her?"

Bert gaped at him, his mouth slowly dropping open. "Actually, about that. She loved it. We'll have to do it again some time." No way in hell could he show weakness or doubt after that interrogation. "Nice coffee by the way."

Still not satisfied, Blake poured the last of the pot into his mug. Shutting off the machine, he leaned against the cabinet to face him. Closing his eyes, he allowed the flow of the room to permeate him. "You probably don't know it, but I can smell the craft on people. I know where you've been, Hubert. Why don't you tell me about your visit to the prison?"

"The prison?" his target stammered. "Oh, um. Well, I just wanted to see how your brother was doing."

Blake glared at him, wondering what the hell Morcant had to do with any of this. Looking him up and down, he realized that would explain the scent. "I'm not really buying that."

Bert rolled his tongue, then slowly got to his feet. "Hey, Blake, I just realized I had an appointment this morning I forgot all about."

"Sit down!" Blake yelled, stepping up to him toe to toe. "You don't leave until I'm satisfied with whatever lies you're going to tell me."

"Lies? Why would I lie to you, Blake?" Perspiration dotted the shorter man's lip. Backing away, he fumbled with the chair, sinking back into it.

"Because my brother isn't the kind of man to trifle with," Blake growled. "So, the question is, which one of us are you more afraid of. Him, or me."

"What's going on in here?" Rider asked in surprise from the doorway.

"Just a friendly visit," Blake replied, his eyes fixed on their guest. He sauntered towards the large table and took a seat on the corner of it. "Hannah came in all beat up this morning. Looks like old Bert's gotten a little too familiar with her. He's forgotten she has friends."

"I haven't forgotten, I swear it." Bert squirmed as Rider noted the empty pot, then took a seat in a chair without his beverage.

"There's plenty upstairs," Blake offered, tossing his head towards the door. "Have a look at her while you're up there. We'll see what you think."

Thirty seconds later, their enforcer burst back into the room. "You did that to her?"

"And he admits he visited my brother," Blake informed him calmly, taking a noisy sip.

"Ok. Guys. The sex was a little rough. I admit, we got a little out of hand, and it won't happen again. Your brother. Yes, I decided to go see him." Bert shrugged. "I wanted to check on him, you know. He used to be a good customer. I figured it was the least I could do."

"Is that the best bullshit you can come up with?" Rider sneered, leaning over the table to glare at him.

"You wouldn't believe the other version," Hubert whispered. "It's better to go with that one."

"What other version?" Blake grunted.

"Morcant took over my body last night and did all those things to Hannah himself, then left me holding the bag," their target blurted all in one breath.

"Finally, something that makes sense. I'll close the store and we'll have a real come to Jesus meeting," Blake informed them, standing to head up the stairs.

TWENTY

Trial by Fire

"EVERYBODY OUT!" Blake hollered, causing all eyes on the sales floor to pivot to him.

"What's going on?" Karen asked from her position at the bookcases.

"Nothing. We've just had a little emergency, and we need to have a team meeting in the basement. Now," Blake snarled, glaring at Hubert, who had followed him. "Don't even think of trying to leave," he barked as the shorter man fidgeted.

"Uh, ok," Karen stammered. Ready to close the sale, she placed the tome they had been discussing in her customer's waiting hands. "I'm sure this book will tell you all you need to know. Step over to the register, and Hannah will be more than happy to wrap it for you."

Turning to Sarah, Blake growled, "Let her ring everyone up, then lock the door and join us downstairs." Turning to the others, he announced, "I need everyone else in the break room in five minutes."

"Why do we have to get everyone out?" Merideth asked doubtfully. "Surely they can still shop."

"No, they can't." He glared at his target. "I'm not sure how sound-proof the floor is."

The color drained from Hubert's face. "Surely you don't mean –"

"Let's go!' Rider pulled him by the arm towards the stairs. "You wanted to be part of our little group. You're going to get your chance."

"But wait, listen…" his voice disappeared as Rider led him away.

"You aren't going to hurt him," Karen stated meekly. "Are you?"

"That depends on what he has to say." Blake ground a fist into the other palm. His eyes fixed on Hannah's face, he could see the bruises beneath her makeup. Cutting his eyes over at Joseline, he clipped, "Are you certain?"

"Yes, I believe so," she whispered, pushing him towards the door to the back. "She's confused about what happened, even if she's standing up for Bert."

"Then we're getting to the bottom of this today!" Grinding his teeth, Blake followed his enforcer, arriving in the basement a moment later.

"I'm making coffee," Rider informed him when the boss arrived.

"Great idea." Blake shook his head, glaring at the man seated at their table.

"Blake, I swear –"

"Save it." Blake's hand shot up, cutting him off. "Let everyone get down here before you go spewing your lies."

"They aren't lies," Bert whispered, looking around at the serene décor. "This room is nice. Very…" he swallowed. "Peaceful."

"Yeah, the torture chamber is next door," Rider boasted, indicating the entrance with a thumb.

A moment later, the girls joined them. "Everyone is gone, and the doors are locked," Sarah stated flatly.

"The blinds and the sign?" Blake poured himself a cup of the fresh brew.

"Off and closed," Hannah added, taking a chair at the table across from her boyfriend. "What's going on?" she mouthed to him.

"What's going on?" Blake snapped, his rage on the thinnest of tethers. Stepping around the table, he grabbed the arms of Hubert's chair, pulling him up and leaning into his face. "This is my coven, and these are my people!" he thundered. "I will not have them abused by the likes of you!"

Across the room, Joseline fidgeted. "Blake, please. He's still my brother."

"Barely," the magister hissed. Slowly righting himself, he indicated the ring of seats. "Everyone sit. Unless we are ready to get down to it."

"I'm ready," Rider sang, opening the door to the next room.

Leaning against the credenza, Karen's eyes swept into the other chamber. She still hadn't gone in there, and from what she saw, she understood why. "You keep some of his equipment," she whispered.

"Some." Blake cocked his head and his necked crackled. "The useful parts. Would you like a tour?" he snapped at Bert.

"No, I...I'm good," the younger man sputtered, cutting his eyes over at Hannah. "I'll tell you anything you want to know."

"He needs to be purified," Rider suggested from the open door. "Then he can talk."

"Yeah," Blake agreed, glancing around at the girls. "The ladies won't have the stomach for it though." Grabbing their target by the chest and arm, he dragged him to his feet. "Let's go, buddy. You girls have some coffee. We'll only be a minute." Shoving Bert through the portal, he slammed the door behind them.

Staring at the wall, Hannah began to cry. "Would someone please tell me what is going on?"

"Hannah, honey." Joseline slipped into the seat next to her, claiming her hands and giving them a squeeze. "Whatever happened to you, it wasn't normal."

"Yes it was!" the girl snapped, yanking the appendages away. "It was consensual, I swear it!"

Taking a chair on the other side, Merideth soothed, "We know you believe that." A scream through the wall shattered the calm.

Fidgeting in her seat, Hannah wanted to flee. "Stop this!"

"We can't," Karen whispered, taking a chair on the other side of the long table as well. "Blake is going to get to the bottom of this. Whatever happens, you can't interrupt."

"Or say anything out of turn," Joseline added, running a hand down Hannah's stiff spine. "Trust us. We aren't going to hurt you."

"Hurt me?" Hannah sniffled. "What about him? What's going on in there?"

Exchanging a circle of glances, none of the girls appeared willing to divulge that detail.

On the other side of the wall, Rider adjusted the straps on Hubert's puny arm. "You need to get to the gym," he scoffed. "Blake is going to have you for lunch."

"Please," Bert begged. "You don't have to do this."

"I'm afraid that we do." Along the far wall, atop a set of short bookcases, Blake adjusted a row of candles. Passing his hand over them, he ignited the tiny flames one by one.

His eyes wide, Bert watched the action. "You're... You're a..."

"Yes, I told you that I'm a witch." The magister sneered. "But you had to go and take my brother's side."

"I didn't have a choice, I swear it!" Hubert pulled against his bonds. Finding them sound, he sniveled. "Please Blake. I didn't want to hurt her. I didn't want to do anything for him!"

"You know what this is?" Toying with the flames, he glanced at their guest. "This is called a trial by fire. We're going to cleanse you, Hubert. Like a newborn babe."

"I'm going to enjoy this," Rider seconded with a twisted grin.

Blake smiled, recalling all the time his enforcer spent avoiding the craft. "I told you it was fun," he teased.

"Are you going to kill me?" Bert's body trembled in his shackles. "Just tell me, please." His face distorted, tears stained his cheeks as Rider ripped open his shirt, exposing his pale, bare chest. Releasing a lever, the wall he was strapped to toggled, tilting into a leaning table. "Oh, God," he screamed.

Lifting one of the wax shafts, Blake carried it over to him. Holding it on its side, the flame lengthened, and wax dripped onto his pink nipple, causing him to bellow in pain.

"Let me scorch his groin," Rider pleaded, holding his hand over the tender area. "Or maybe shove something up his ass."

"Please, no," Hubert begged. Scrunching his butt cheeks, he tightened the muscles without any hope of protecting the delicate region.

Continuing to drip the wax, Blake let it cool, then picked it off to apply another layer. "For every scar she carries, you will have one to match." Righting the candle, he applied the back of his hand, turning Bert's cheeks bright red. Adding a few extra swings, he grimaced at the blood oozing from his fattened lips. "Bring the blades," he commanded, returning the flame to its stand with the others.

Turning to one of the cabinets, Rider produced a flat wooden box. Placing it on the table next to the harness, he opened it and stepped out of the way. On one side, small prongs held a variety of cutting devices in place. Sharp pointed instruments designed to mark their victims and inflict agony.

"I swear to you, I didn't want it," Hubert groveled, only able to see a portion of the container. "Please don't do this to me."

"Did she beg?" Blake demanded, selecting one of the wooden shafts and testing the shiny tip on an extended finger. When no response came, he shouted, "Did she beg! When you had her tied to that bed?"

"Yes!" Hubert screamed back, his body wracked with sobs. "Yes, she cried. I didn't know. I couldn't stop him!" He broke down into incoherent babble, pleas and excuses interchanging.

"But you agreed to help him," Rider insisted.

"Yes. When I saw him at the prison. He told me he wanted Hannah. I didn't see how he could have her, so I agreed. He was trapped there. How would he possibly?" His body continued to shake. "Just kill me," he bellowed, rocking his full length side to side. "I deserve it." His head rolling forward to hang over his battered chest, he sobbed, his words muffled.

Looking at his partner, Blake shrugged. "Do you think he's had enough?"

"I didn't even get to burn him," Rider observed.

"Well, here." Blake offered the blade. "You can cut him."

Staring at it, Rider shook his head, then pulled on the

lever. Laying the table down flat, he selected a bowl of water and a towel, replacing the set of tools on the table with them.

Releasing one of the straps, Blake barked, "Clean yourself up. We'll be waiting for you outside."

"You think he'll end it?" Rider asked when they had shut the door, safely on the other side.

"End what?" Joseline snapped, fidgeting in her seat.

"He won't," Blake soothed, moving to the head of the table. "Give him a few minutes to right himself and he'll join us. Then we'll get the truth."

"The truth?" Karen coughed. "What the hell were you doing in there?"

Rider stuck out his lips, giving her a shrug. "Softening him up?"

"I can't believe you kept Morcant's little torture chamber," Sarah hissed, leaning towards him.

"There are some things you can't achieve by words," Blake replied flatly. "Now, I believe our guest will be ready to talk."

TWENTY-ONE

To Be Worthy

EVENTUALLY, the door opened, and Hubert stumbled out. His shirt hung open, gaping where Rider had ripped away the buttons. Grasping the edges, he folded it across his wounded chest, then ran his fingers through his mussed hair. Looking up at Blake at the far end of the table, he shivered, selecting the empty chair next to Rider, who sat nearer to him.

"Dear God," Hanna breathed, taking him in.

"He is perfectly fine," Blake stated calmly. "Aren't you, Hubert."

"Yes. Yes, I'm fine," the other man agreed through his swollen lips. His eyes darted around at the circle of friends, each with their cup of coffees and smug expressions.

"Are you ready to talk?" Sarah asked, scrunching in her seat to get a look at the downturned face.

Bert nodded. "What do you want to know?"

"Just start at the beginning," Blake instructed, having a noisy sip.

"The beginning," Bert echoed thoughtfully. "Well, I guess that would be a few years ago. It started out really simple," he explained, waving his bruised arms. "I made a delivery to M & J's on a particular day. Morc was in the mood to chat, so we had a visit. Perfectly innocent."

He glanced around again, wiping his face, but avoiding his burning mouth. "I liked the things that he told me. About the shop and about his magic. I thought most of it was bullshit, but you know… So, after that, I made a point of talking to him when I brought in a few boxes. Then he gave me a quest."

"A quest?" Karen stared at him, wide eyed.

"Yeah. It was a simple little thing. Like an errand. It got me excited." He fidgeted in his seat again. "After that, I even faked orders when he hadn't placed any. Just so I could stop by here to see him."

"You did what?" Joseline growled. "He wasn't really buying all those candles?"

"Uh, no," Bert clipped, his eyes flicking at her and then away, anxiously. "I dumped them."

"Oh, you didn't," she seethed.

"Sorry, Sis."

"Don't sorry Sis me!" She placed her palms flat on the table, pushing herself up. Catching her arm, Blake waved her to sit.

"It's ok," he whispered. "Let him finish."

Retaking her seat, she growled, "Later then."

Cupping his hands, Hubert toyed with his fingers. "Anyway, I liked coming here. Morc made me feel special. I wasn't really part of the coven, but he said that was important. He needed someone on the outside."

"When was this? Before he went to prison?" Blake asked curiously.

"Oh, yes. Months before. So, when it all went down, no

one was more surprised than me. But as soon as he was sentenced, I went to see him."

"In the middle of COVID?" Meri asked. "I didn't think they allowed visitors."

"Well, they didn't," he confirmed. "But Morcant can be rather…convincing. He got some of the guards, I guess you could say, persuaded. He sent me a letter requesting some of the books from here in the shop."

"You stole them!" Sarah whispered, recalling the missing tomes.

"It wasn't stealing," he denied with a shrug. "They belonged to him, after all. I just retrieved them for him. And delivered them to the prison."

"And then he started cursing people," Rider concluded, thinking of May. "What else did he do?"

"I really have no idea," Burt replied airily, opening a palm towards him. "I didn't ask." He swallowed.

"So how does Hannah fit in to all this?" Blake asked, directing them back to their target.

"Well, first there was Joseline," Bert explained. "He told me you guys would come looking for her." He raised his shoulders slowly, slouching. "Well, not for her exactly. He told me I should ensure you acquired what you seek. I was so mad when I realized it was my sister."

Joseline's features softened, her anger ebbing a bit as she glanced at her half-siblings.

"It was his curse on our mother that prompted the search," Merideth recalled quietly.

"He's had this planned for a while," Blake agreed, studying Sarah. "Converting you to Brenna was only part of his plan."

"Doing what?" Hubert asked, his brow furrowed in confusion.

"That's a long story," Sarah supplied. "Are we up to Hannah now?"

"Yeah, I guess we are." Hubert nodded. "I met her at Madam Demore's place. I was keeping the business running while Joseline was off playing around with you guys. She seemed nice, so we had a few dates. Then I introduced her to you guys, and you gave her a job here. When I went for another visit, Morc got really excited. He told me he wanted to induct her into our 'new' coven. I told him to be my guest."

"You gave him permission, just like that," Blake snarled.

"Well, yeah. I told you I didn't see how he would manage it. But when it happened, I knew something was wrong. I could feel him creeping into my body. Moving me. Controlling me." He shivered violently in the chair. "The next thing I knew, I was watching it all. Through my eyes, of course, but unable to alter what was happening."

Hannah began to cry, sobbing loudly. "I thought it was you! I thought you wanted me that way." She wailed, and Joseline shoved a box of tissues across to her. "I let you do all of those things to me for *nothing*."

"At least now you know it wasn't him," Blake consoled.

"I doubt that helps," Sarah chimed in, recalling her own experience. Catching Hannah's gaze, she smiled gently at her. "I know it's hard to believe now, but eventually this will get better. Morcant raped me through a dream. It's how he initiated his spell, or curse, upon me," she explained in a hushed tone. "I had nightmares about it for a long time."

Joseline fidgeted in her chair. "That man is a menace. He enjoys coercing women to lay with him."

"It gives him power," Blake added. "The negative energy feeds him." His mind briefly leapt to Julia, the mother of his son. Forcing the thought away, he couldn't go there.

Returning to the present, he leaned back in his chair. "Now the real question is, what to do with you?"

"Do with me?" Hubert stammered, his eyes darting about him. "I just told you everything. That's what you wanted. What do you mean *do* with me?"

Rider snickered. "We're not Morcant. We aren't dumping your body anywhere if that's what you're thinking."

"Thank God for that," Karen seconded, fidgeting in her seat.

"I think they should join the coven," Merideth suggested, earning a dark glance from Blake. "What?" She scowled. "You said your brother let mortals in."

"Yes, so he could use them," Blake pointed out, indicating Hubert with an open palm. "Case in point."

"Yeah, but they already know everything that's going on," Karen seconded.

"Exactly. That makes them susceptible to my brother's influence," their magister insisted.

"Uh-uh. No way," Bert thrust his arms across his chest, then winced. "I'm finished with that guy. He can kill me, but I'm not doing anything else for him."

Sniffling, Hannah nodded. "I always wanted to be a part of the craft. I loved the way my Auntie used her gift to help people." A few tears escaped, and she dabbed at them with trembling fingers. "If I join you, does that mean I get to help punish him? For what he did?" She looked at Blake, her lip trembling.

Sensing her anguish, Joseline pleaded, "Please, Blake. We can't shut them out after all that's happened. It would be cruel."

Blake thrust his hand up, stopping her there. "It will be dangerous. You have no real power to protect yourselves."

"We could teach them," Sarah offered. "I'm a bit of a caster."

"And I know some curses," Rider seconded.

Raising his arms in surrender, Blake sighed. "All in favor?"

Hands went up around the group, no one dissenting. "Well, I guess you're in. Congrats," he scoffed, rising from his chair, and strolling out of the room.

TWENTY-TWO

None of This

BLAKE STOOD IN HIS KITCHEN, bare chested and staring aimlessly into his fridge.

"Look, Father!" Matthew squealed, pointing out the back door to the patio. "It's snowing outside."

Blake closed the appliance and ambled over to stand behind him. Pushing the curtain aside, he glared at the curls of fluff. "It can't be. It's too early yet for a good snow." But the flakes were falling, taking his breath away.

"See, Father!" Matt bounced with excitement. "We have a holiday next week. The ground will be white, and we will have so much fun."

"Do you like the snow, Matty? Were you hoping that it would come?" Blake rested his hand on the small head before him, the warmth tingling his fingers as he brushed the dark hair.

"Oh, yes, Father! Will you play with me when it's fluffy?"

"What will we play when the snow is ready?" Blake studied him as he spoke, his tiny hands demonstrating their games.

"We'll build a snowman. One as big as me." The boy giggled, delighted at the prospect. "And we can make snowballs to throw in fights." He imitated with his arm. "And I'll have a cave to hide in, so no one can smack me."

Blake hid his fears behind a broad smile. "We'll see, my son. First it would need to snow for a few hours, or even days, for us to have that much fun."

"It will, Father," Matthew assured. Breathing heavily, he frosted the glass, then smudged it with his fingers. His eyes bright, confidence exuded around him.

"But it is not time for that kind of snow," Blake persisted, his face growing grim. "We mustn't interfere with the nature of things, even if we can. It harms our world. It harms those we care about. When we meddle."

Matthew's smile disappeared. Slowly, he raised to his eyes to the man next to him. "Yes, Father," he whispered.

"Matty!" Ezamay called from the top of the stairs. "Time for bed, my precious."

Standing straight, his son smiled. "I have to go, Father. Grammy is calling."

Pursing his lips, Blake watched him scurry away, Joseline and Karen sauntering past him as they entered the familiar kitchen. Locking eyes with Josee, Blake huffed a puff of disgusted air. Opening the door, he fled to the patio, closing it behind him.

Moving to the edge of the narrow covering, cold air blasted his bare chest, hardening his nipples in defense. Flakes of ice swirled before him, floating to the ground. When the door opened, Joseline alone invaded his space.

"I wish to speak to you, magister," she announced, closing the portal, then slowly moving towards him.

"About?" He looked up at the dark clouds above, his mind still on the boy.

"About my brother. There is something I need to know about the other day."

"Something?" he scoffed. "There are many things I'd like to know."

Arriving next to him, she wrapped her jacket around her. "Aren't you cold?" she demanded, looking him up and down.

"Not half as cold as I feel on the inside," he confessed quietly.

Sensing his despondence, like cracks in his soul, anger filled the gaps. "I need to know why you did it," she snapped, ready to confront him. "Why did you torture my brother?" She glared at his profile, steeling herself for his rage. When he didn't reply, she pushed. "Why did you torture Hubert, Blake?"

"It was like a cleansing. It had to be done," he replied flatly. "I had to know."

"To know what? He had already told you Morcant had used his body. It wasn't his fault –"

"Do not be naive, Joseline." He pivoted, facing her squarely. "When you take the side of such a cruel man. When your choice is made. You deserve to be punished."

"You were his judge then. Making certain Bert saw retribution for following Morcant." She glared at him, struggling to understand.

"I had to purify him of my brother's influence," Blake snapped. "How else could he be allowed to remain among us?"

Her breathing shallow, her eyes grew wide. "You wanted to kill him."

"Yes. For what he did, he deserved a swift death," Blake hissed, towering over her. "But I had to be sure. And I had to be fair." He looked her up and down.

"You spared him on my account," she whispered. "You

were using him to test me," she concluded. "I let you do that to him."

"And you passed," he growled. Taking a step back, he gave her some room. Returning his gaze to the drifting snow, he inhaled deeply. "We should have a meeting. I fear we must make our move against Morcant."

"I'll summon the others," she said softly, her heart broken within her chest. Pausing, she said quietly, "What would you have done? If I had stood against you, that day." She felt the pain wash over him, his hand swiping quickly at the tear that dripped onto his cheek.

"I always do what I must, dear Joseline," he whispered. "No matter what it costs me."

Leaving him, she entered the house. Karen and Sarah sat at the table, enjoying cups of a warm drink. "Gather everyone. We must have a meeting, right away."

"Is he going to stay out there?" Karen asked, indicating their leader with a stiff digit. "He'll fucking freeze like that!"

"He has a fire within to keep him warm," Joseline clipped. Going through the living room and down the hall, she knocked lightly on Merideth's door.

"Come in!" A voice sang on the other side.

Cracking the portal, Josee poked her head inside. At the table, the couple sat with mugs and smiles. "We're having a meeting in a few minutes. There's no dress code, but I suggest you bring your coats."

"Coats." Rider frowned. "Why?"

"Blake's out on the patio." Joseline indicated the direction with a toss of her head. "If we have to meet outside, it's a bit chilly."

"He's been moody as fuck ever since the Hannah and Bert thing," he muttered, then slurped his drink. "Are they coming?"

"I spoke to her just a bit ago, and yes they are on their way, as soon as she gets the shop closed." Merideth provided.

"Good. Then the two of you should prepare yourselves and come out when you are ready," Joseline suggested, closing the door behind her.

"Prepare ourselves," Meri said quietly. "What do you suppose this is going to be about?"

"The darkness that lies ahead, one can only presume," Rider replied quietly. Cutting his eyes over at her, he grimaced. "Blake is becoming unstable, Boo. I'm afraid of what comes next."

The group assembled in the living room, bringing out chairs from the kitchen to form a circle around the coffee table. Blake's chair at one end, Merideth looked at the arrangement and shivered.

"What's wrong?" Rider asked, sliding his arm around her.

"It's like the grouping in the store," she whispered. "The one Morcant used. I think it must have been something like this, with his followers surrounding him."

"It's just a meeting." Rider shrugged. "Don't let it bother you, Boo."

But it did bother her. Visions haunted her day and night as of late. Everything held a meaning behind it, and it terrified her. Rubbing her arms briskly, she forced herself to sit in one of the straight-backed chairs so that Rider would be next to her, on the right, keeping Blake's seat at the far end and away from her.

When Hubert and Hannah arrived, the last speck of sunlight had gone from the sky. Stomping their feet to remove the light dusting of snow, the couple hung their coats on the rack next to the front door. Bert looked over anxiously at the circle of friends. Taking Hannah's hand, they presented themselves together. "Hi, guys," he breathed.

"Have a seat," Blake growled, joining them from outside via the kitchen. Still half naked, he ran his fingers through the hair that spread across his bare chest.

"Here, honey." Sarah offered him a white button up shirt. "I think everyone would be more comfortable," she added, smiling up at him.

"What do I care for comfort," he growled. However, he accepted the covering. Shoving his arms in, he fastened the sleeves. Then, starting at the top, he buttoned the third one and worked his way down from there, moving through the grouping as he did so. Sitting, a sprig of hair still exposed at the top of the V, he glared at them.

"You do not look well, magister," Meri said quietly, glad she had kept some distance between them. She hid herself from him, with Bert and then Hannah between.

"I don't look well," Blake clipped, glaring at her. "And how am I supposed to look?"

"Better than you do now," Karen seconded. "Who needs Morcant to terrify them when we have you."

The others laughed anxiously. Blake only scowled. "Do you think that is funny? Do you think my brother plotting and moving against us is a joke?"

"No," she replied softly.

"Good," he snapped, his eyes scanning the group. "Because it won't be." Digging in his pocket, he pulled out his copy of the list. Unfolding it, he leaned over, smoothing it against the dark wood table. "There's something missing on this list," he announced. "Something we forgot. Something we didn't write down."

"I thought we remembered it all, sweetheart," Sarah replied, leaning over to have a look. "Are you sure we missed one?"

"I'm certain." He glanced at her tense features, then around his circle of followers again. This time, he grimaced. "I'm sorry," he offered. "I know I ask much of you." His eyes met Joseline's, and he nodded. "I have tested each of you in one way or another and found you all worthy."

"Oh, thank God," Bert mumbled, adjusting in his seat. Still holding his hand, Hannah grinned at him.

"I'm surprised you two are still together," Rider observed from the other comfy chair. He glanced at the three women on the sofa, Sarah on Blake's end, Karen on his, and Joseline in the center. "Would you stay with a man who had done that to you?"

"He didn't do that to me," Hannah defended. "Morcant did."

"And he did it to me, too," Bert stuttered, his voice unsteady. "We were both victims that night."

"And you want a little revenge." Blake sneered. "You think a little anger will sustain you."

"Well, he's in prison," Bert quibbled. "What can we do?"

"I've paid a guard well for his services," Blake informed them, sitting back against his cushions. "He has provided information so far. I'm going to ask him to settle this. To arrange for my brother's demise and see that he never leaves there alive."

Sarah gasped. "Why would you do that?"

"Because!" Blake nearly shouted. "I'm tired of him jabbing at us from out of the darkness. Stabbing and injuring us at will."

"You'll get the man killed." Joseline panted, her chest heaving. "We can't attack him in such a place."

"She's right," Rider agreed. "We need him out. In the open, that we can get at him."

"I don't see how that would be wise. To remain in this war that cannot be won." He indicated the page before them. He glanced at the stairs, the light on in his son's room. "I fear what is to come if we do not act." Lowering his gaze, he stared at Merideth. "Tell us, seer. I know your vision is strong."

Meri fidgeted, her chair creaking. Licking her lips, she flicked her eyes around at the others, meeting each in turn as they stared at her. "I've seen many things as of late," she whispered. "I cannot say which of them are true." She lifted her chin, studying her sister, her understanding of the craft so much greater than when she first joined Blake's coven. "Some of us are going to die," she stated flatly.

"That's comforting," Rider snapped. Sitting up straight, he held up his open palms. "How does this help, exactly?"

"We must know what we face," Josee defended. "We must each deal with the fear inside us."

Blake's features twisted into a horrible grin. "Someone has figured it out. Why my brother is so powerful. Perhaps I am not the only whisperer."

Karen pulled her legs beneath her, sitting crookedly upon them and rubbing the exposed calf. "Are you going to share with the rest of us?" she asked in bewilderment.

"He uses our emotions against us," Sarah suggested, shifting her gaze between them. "In my nightmare. The night he unleashed his spell upon me, he covered my eyes. The whole time, I couldn't see him. All I could do was feel what he was doing to me." She swallowed. "That made it so much worse."

"Are you suggesting he did what he did, because it was the things I was afraid of most?" Hannah shivered, her wounds fresh in her mind.

Hubert nodded. "He controlled me. And I watched it

happen. I felt powerless to stop it." He squeezed her hand. "I have to admit, that might be the greatest fear of any man."

"And if he can do this to us now, imagine what he will do if he ever gets out," Blake suggested, tapping their witch's warning. "If we don't get a handle on all of this, none of this is going to matter."

"Well, we can't take him on until he is freed," Rider stated firmly. "I won't ask your guard to take on such an endeavor." A mumble of agreement swept the circle.

Nodding, Blake sighed. "All right. We will wait. But winter is upon us."

"The holiday season is upon us," Ezamay corrected as she joined them. Perching on the arm of Rider's chair between him and her daughter, she smiled. "We can use the warmth of this time to fortify ourselves."

Blake glanced at the room, its door closed. "He's asleep?"

"Yes." May gave a single nod of her old head.

"What are you reading to him?" her magister asked. "He seemed quite excited about it."

"I'm not actually reading anything. I've been telling him stories. Sharing about the time when I was a girl, and the witches of the past." She smiled, the memories sweet to recollect.

"You've been telling him about the craft," Blake whispered, his understanding clearer. "You must stop this."

"Stop?" Sarah sat up straighter. "I thought we were going to teach him, love."

Blake shrugged, bobbling his head. His hands had been folded before him as he leaned, elbows to knees. Raising his index fingers to a point, he indicated the patio and garden beyond. "I think he has brought the snow," he confessed. "When he first came to this house, I caught no scent of the craft upon him. Now, I sense it growing stronger every day.

One day, and maybe soon, he will be a powerful witch. Maybe even more powerful than me," he whispered.

"What rubbish!" Ezamay cackled. "He is but a boy. What power could he have? He is much too young, Judoc."

Blake cut his eyes over at Joseline. "How old were you?"

"Young." She coughed, shifting anxiously in her seat between the girls. "I'm not sure of my age, but I remember how being around the other children affected me. I soaked their emotions like a sponge, reflecting them back with immense veracity."

Blake cut his eyes back to May. "Now, imagine that you can make things happen. When you want something, you can bring it into fruition." He shifted the gaze to Rider, then Merideth. "What were you doing, the day the two of you reconciled?"

"We were...painting. We had watercolors in the kitchen." Merideth smiled fondly "The three of us were enjoying the morning. We had lunch. And then we had a nap." She grinned, her mother's form blocking her view of Rider, but she knew he as there. "Was that the gist of it, Boo?"

"I have to admit, I was a little surprised. I didn't think we were getting along that well," Rider said quietly. "But she went and put that ring on, and I knew we had things to discuss."

"Are you suggesting that Matthew caused this?" Sarah gasped, making the connection.

"Not on purpose." Blake unfolded his hands to sit back in his chair. "But I think he desired a reconciliation between you. He cares very deeply for you. For all within our coven." He bobbed his head slowly, sweeping the arc of them. "If he sensed the two of you suffering. That each of you secretly wished...he used his gift to make it so."

"If this is true, then he needs more, not less!" Ezamay stood, pacing around the group. "We must train him, and quickly. Each of us sharing all that we can with him, guiding him in the path he should walk. If he is free to choose his own way..." her voice faded as she considered the possibility. "Darkness will claim him if we do not set his feet firmly within the light."

The magister nodded, considering her argument. "And so it shall be. I want him to spend time with each of us. Share your talents. Explain to him the choices you make and why the path you take is for the goodness of others." Blake stood. "He is one of us, in practice at least. In our care, we must do our best not to fail him."

"But what about Morcant?" Karen asked. "He will use Matthew against us, I'm sure."

"We cannot allow that to happen," Merideth whispered. Tears in her eyes, she blinked rapidly, her eye drawn to the ring she had been drawn to wear. "He is a precious child, and the evil of Morcant must never be allowed to reach him." She looked over at Rider, who nodded.

"Then we need to get the store staffed," Sarah pointed out. "Because we are all going to be too busy being witches to worry about selling trinkets and candles."

Blake smiled at her, feeling more like his old self already. "Thank you, pumpkin."

"For what?" she asked. Standing beside him, she stretched, her full belly pushed out before her.

"For being here. You are all an integral part of our coven. We need each of us to do our part, and to look out for each other." He smiled, inhaling deeply. "Gosh, I feel like I've just come out of a slumber." He offered her his hand, then Hannah the other.

Rising, Hannah accepted the appendage. "Is this some

kind of ritual thing?" she asked anxiously. "We haven't learned any real magic yet."

"Sure you have." He winked at her as the rest joined them, the hands linking into a ring. "You see this?" He held up their connection on both sides. "This is an unbreakable bond. As long as we have it, my brother can never tear us apart."

TWENTY-THREE

Master Korrigan

STANDING at the small desk in his bedroom, Blake pulled the envelope out of the pile, noting the return address. "Holy shit. It came."

Finding scissors in the middle drawer, he cut the end off so as not to damage the precious document inside. Sliding it out, he unfolded it and stared at the page, running his thumb lightly over his son's name. "And it only cost me five hundred dollars for forged proof that he belongs to me," he muttered to the empty space around him. He would have paid many times that.

Taking the page, he strolled down the hall and made a left, into the main corridor. Only two bedrooms lay in that section, between the junction and the stairs, both on the right, as the left opened to the great room below.

The first an empty room, it sat waiting, and they would deal with it in a few weeks. And next to that, the one his son had chosen the night Merideth first cared for him on their wedding day.

Pausing in the door, Blake inhaled deeply, his son's scent filling the newly decorated space. Seated at a table sized for his small body, the boy drew on a large blank page, adding splashes of color wherever it pleased him. "Oh, Rider," he mumbled. "I'm not sure he's ready for that yet." Stepping inside, he announced, "I got a surprise today I wish to share with you before bed."

Looking up at him with wide blue eyes, Matthew asked with a perfectly straight face, "Is it chocolate?"

Blake coughed a laugh, caught off guard. Taking a tiny chair, his massive frame squatted onto it, scooting up to the flat surface. "No, it isn't chocolate," he managed. "The state granted our change to your birth certificate." He unfolded it so Matt could read his own name.

"That's me," the boy whispered. Looking up at his father, he smiled.

"And this is me." Blake pointed at his name now located in the proper box.

"Jud-uck. Joo-duck." Matty pronounced it a couple of ways, unsure which to settle on. "But your name is Blake."

"Well, people call me Blake, and I like that. But my legal name is Judoc Korrigan. I have held that moniker for many years. And now, officially, your name is also Korrigan, as you are part of my family and my line."

"Huh." Matthew returned to his art as Sarah quietly sidled up to the door, out of sight so she could listen.

"Do you know what this means?" Blake asked, shaking the page lightly. The lack of a reply did not detour his explanation. "This is a birth certificate. This is how the state tells people who you are and who your parents are. With my name on here, no one can ever take you away from me." His voice cracked, the moment lost on the seven-year-old. "Of course, it also tells me you are having a birthday soon."

"I'll be eight," Matthew informed him proudly, still

focused on his creation. Then he paused to look at him. "Did the state put Sarah's name on my certificate?"

"Oh," Blake paused, his lips puckered. "Well, you do ask some hard questions. No, son. A birth certificate is for the parents who made you."

"So will they take me away when you die?"

Outside, Sarah gasped, covering her mouth in grief at the very thought of either instance occurring.

"Oh, Matty," Blake whispered. His son didn't understand at all. He carefully folded the page. "You are Matthew Korrigan, and this mansion belongs to our family. I have lived here all my life. And you will as well, if you so desire it. No one can take that from you."

"They took me away from momma's house when she died," Matthew pushed. "Grandpa Charlie said I couldn't stay there anymore."

"Did he live there with you? Is he Julia's father?" They hadn't given him any details on his son's past, and so far his searches had turned up little to nothing.

Matt shrugged. "He stayed across the street. He's a nice man with a wrinkly black face."

"Oh." Blake sat up straight in his chair. "Grandpa Charlie was a neighbor." Perhaps Julia had not gone home to her family. Or she had no family to go to. "Well, no one will take you from here. And no, Sarah's name is not on your birth certificate, but maybe some day we can get a different kind of document that will name her as your mother."

"I like Meri," Matty announced. "She makes me sandwiches." He chewed his crayon. "But Sarah is a nice mommy. And she lets me touch her tummy." His eyes grew wide. "She has a baby in there," he whispered.

"Yes, she does." Blake snickered. "Soon we will prepare

the room next door, and when it is born, he or she will sleep next to you. So, you will have to watch out for our baby."

"Will your name be on the baby certificate?"

"Why yes it will." Blake grinned down at him proudly. "And Sarah's name will be, too. We made our new baby together."

"Where does Merdith's name go?"

Blake sighed, his eyes tearing up. "Meri's name goes on your heart, son. Because she loves you very much." Realizing most of what they had said was over his son's head, he gave the young man a pat on the back, then stood. "You are a bright little guy, and I'm so glad I have the chance to share your life." Looking over the drawing from above, he shook his head. "Have you had your bath?"

"Yes, Father."

"Then it's time for bed. Let me tuck you in," he suggested, leaning over to scoop the crayons into their box.

Dropping the one in his hand, Matthew scampered over to climb beneath his covers. "Will Sarah come and read my story?"

Blake glanced at the selection of books that adorned his new shelves. "If she doesn't, and you are still awake in half an hour, I'll read you one," he promised. Bending over, he kissed him gently on the forehead. "Good night, Master Korrigan."

"Good night...Daddy." Matty whispered back, giving Blake's heart a flutter.

Snapping off the light on the way out, Blake stepped into the hall, coming face to face with Sarah. "Uh, hi." He glanced over his shoulder at the boy. "How long have you been here?"

"Long enough." She smiled up at him, placing her hands on his chest as she leaned against him. "I'm so proud to be your wife. And to carry your child, Judoc Korrigan."

Wrapping her, he breathed into her flame red hair. "This is a wonderful day."

Slipping from his grasp, she caught his hand and tugged him down the hall, back towards the junction. "I wish it was all good news, love."

Still carrying the birth certificate, he followed. Inside their bedroom, he opened a drawer for special papers and slipped it inside. "Well, don't be coy about it. What catastrophe faces us now?" His eyes on the desk, he caught a glimpse of another envelope from the state. This one from the parole board. "Oh, no," he gasped, his fingers trembling when he picked it up. "Empty. Where's the letter?"

She held it out, offering it to him. "We have a week," she declared gently. "They are releasing him on the twenty third."

"Before Christmas," he surmised. "We need to tell the others."

"They have granted me a restraining order, for all the good it will do. He isn't allowed near me, this house as my primary residence, or the store, where I work." Her eyes grew misty at the idea of looking over her shoulder everywhere she went.

"Don't," Blake challenged, pulling her against him. "You will never be alone. Rider or I will go every where that you go. I promise."

Clinging to him, Sarah blinked back her tears, hoping his plan would be enough to protect her from the evil she could feel coming her way.

Epilogue

"OH MY GOD, I never thought they would leave us alone," Blake panted. Pulling a tall chair up next to her bed, he grunted, "Let me see her."

Holding their baby in her arms, Sarah grinned at him. "You were making everyone nervous with all that pacing you were doing."

"Well, I was anxious. New dads get to be a little nervous."

Her smile lessened, she sighed. "I wish that's all that had been driving your steps."

"I don't want to talk about him," Blake snarled. Pulling at the blanket, he managed to free a tiny fist. "There she is!"

"Baby, we haven't seen or heard from him since his release three weeks ago. Is there a chance he has run off to a new life and will leave us alone?"

"None," he clipped. "We must never let our guard down, precious. My brother will come for us, I assure you. But right now, I just want to see my princess."

Relenting, Sarah pulled at the blanket, opening it so he could count all the fingers and toes. "She's all there, I promise. And since we waited to learn the sex, now we have to choose a name."

"Wow. She's incredible, Sarah." He gasped, her belly soft as he inspected the clamped cord.

"Are you disappointed?" Her green eyes grew misty.

"Me? Never! We've made a beautiful daughter, pumpkin. And a powerful witch she will be in her time," he promised. Holding a tiny foot, his thumb lightly caressed the curve of her heel.

"How is it we are always powerful? I never hear you describe anyone as a puny little thing."

"Well, I assure you there are some pitiful ones out there." He laughed, curling the cover back around the treasured little body. "Let's name her Amber. Amberlynn Sage."

"ASK?" Sarah giggled, unable to control her amusement.

He shrugged. "They're just initials." He blinked at her, a bit somber. "Sage was my Aunt Abby's middle name. Her initials were ASK."

"Oh," Sarah breathed. "I didn't know. You want to honor her."

He sighed. "I think it is fitting that we pay a little homage to the past." He collected a tiny fist, splaying the fingers to stroke them. A tear dropped onto his cheek. "I'm going to go call the house and tell them she's here."

"Don't be long. Amberlynn Sage and I will be testing out the tit feeding."

He chuckled. "Tit feeding." Kissing her forehead, he left them to it as he sauntered out of the room.

Thank You

Thank you for sharing in this magical adventure! Please be sure to leave a review and don't miss the next installment of the Unexpected Magic Series ~ Sam

Books in this series include:
> The Binding (book 1)
> The Wicked Awakened (book 2)
> The Secret Sibling (book 3)
> The Whisperer (book 4)
> The Magister's Child (book 5)

Boxed Sets
> The Unexpected Magical Opening Duo (books 1 and 2)

About the Author

Anyone who knows me could tell you, I am a friendly kind of person, never met a stranger and take up conversations anywhere at any time. I work hard, and my mind never seems to shut down, as I wake up often in the middle of the night with ideas pouring out and demanding to be dealt with. Of course that means much of my books were written in the middle of the night.

I grew up and still live in the great state of Texas where everything is bigger, where we have warm weather and a central location. I love my state, my town, and my family, which includes my four sons, my significant other, and many friends as well.

I have thoroughly enjoyed writing this story and hope that you will love reading it just as much. And of course, there will be many more adventures to come.

You can follow Samantha Jacobey at:
Website: www.SamJacobey.com
Facebook: https://www.facebook.com/SamJacobey
Twitter: https://twitter.com/SamJacobey

Also by SAMANTHA JACOBEY

https://www.lavishpublishing.com/authors/samantha-jacobey/

A New Life Series – an epic adventure, TORI FARRELL's life IS one wild story... escaped from a biker gang and running from drug lords... used by the FBI and hoping to protect her present from her past... IT'S DARK - IT'S BRUTAL, and it's WORTH EVERY MINUTE OF IT!! (Mature read, 18+ for graphic sexual content and violence, including rape)

Irrevocable Series – Armageddon through the eyes of an entitled seventeen-year-old, BAILEY DEWITT's life has become a broken mess... after her parents died unexpectedly, she didn't think it could get any worse. But when the arrogance of man catches up and puts the entire world into a dooms-day spiral, there will be only one place she can run to - the one place she wanted desperately to escape. Can she and Caleb build a life together when the world is falling apart? (New Adult)

Teach Me to Prey – in this standalone thriller, JASON TRUITT and his friends have gotten their way for years. Deceit, sex, and foul play aren't normally covered in the curriculum, but they're doing whatever it takes to get under BECKY STEWART's skin. When one of the boys turns up dead, it's a race against time to save the others; a STUNNING STORY that will get your heart racing and leave you breathless by the end… (New Adult)

Sweet Christmas Series - Life isn't always sweet, even for girls called Candy. Candice Parker's life has never been easy. Plagued by losses and setbacks, each day is a struggle for the petite brunette and her young son. When fireman Gary enters her world, he is one mistake she refuses to make; but after tragedy strikes, she may not have a choice. (New Adult)

Also From The Lavish Family

Fairfield Corners Series

L.A. Remenicky

https://www.lavishpublishing.com/authors/l-a-remenicky/

Small town romance with a paranormal twist! Each in standalone style, read and enjoy any order, any number!

Saving Cassie – Book 1: Some secrets are too dangerous to keep.

After ten years in the big city, Cassie Holt is back in Fairfield Corners. She may look like the same girl who left home a decade before but she's hiding a dark truth from everyone. When her life is threatened by the demons of her past, her best friend—who happens to be the local sheriff—offers his help.

Deputy Logan Miller has been burned by love. He's not looking to get involved but duty calls when the sheriff tasks him with Cassie's protection. Thrown into close quarters with the gorgeous bookseller, sparks fly. Logan is drawn to Cassie, but it's hard to get close to someone who keeps themselves guarded all the time.

To keep Cassie safe, Logan must open his heart but that's something he swore he'd never do.

Ragan's Song – Book 2: One look into his eyes told her she was in trouble – again!

Ragan returned home to celebrate her parent's anniversary hoping they would forgive her the secrets she's kept from them over the last few years. When she discovered that Adam was still living in Fairfield Corners she hoped her secrets were safe, secrets that drove her away three years, secrets that could change both their lives forever.

Adam Bricklin was devastated when Ragan Newlin left town. No note, no email, no text. She was just gone. It has taken three years for Adam to finally move past the heartbreak he suffered when Ragan left town. Now he's moved on and everything was going well until the day Ragan returned to Fairfield Corners. Now the melody that he lost all those years ago is back. It's the same tune he heard that tells him right from wrong—the one that sang Ragan was the one.

Even separation can't silence Adam and Ragan's song, and now that she's back it's time for Adam to decide if he should let the song die or breathe life into it once again.

Where There's Faith – Book 3: A past she can't remember. A love he can't forget.

After losing everything in an accident that he can only blame himself for, Robbie Newlin embraced sobriety and tried to live his life quietly alone at this family's cottage on the lake. Grief being his only ally, Robbie was perfectly content with how he lived until Faith moved into the cottage next door. Now Faith had him questioning whether to keep grieving or to open his broken heart to let love in again.

Faith McMillan had no memory of her life before that day three years ago. The physical scars had faded but the emotional ones were still fresh and raw. Living rent-free seemed like a great way to finish her second book and give her the time to figure out her next move, but then she met the reclusive guy next door and everything changed.

To get past the broken parts, Robbie and Faith must figure out if they want to continue living their lives in solitude or take a chance on finding an ending together.

Behind Blue Eyes Series
Sara J. Bernhardt
https://www.lavishpublishing.com/authors/sara-j-bernhardt/

A father's desire to save his child presents him with an unthinkable choice that leaves him darker than human, forced to roam through time alone as he searches for the place he belongs.

Adam Gold – Book 1: Fleeing the French invasion of Geneva Switzerland in the 1700s, Adam Gold books passage to America with his family. On the ship, Adam's daughter falls fatally ill. A mysterious man comes to Adam with a way to save his child by turning Adam into something darker than human.

The Medallion – Book 2: Adam Gold, an immortal with sweet eyes of blue, rushes through the centuries on a quest for reason and a thirst for revenge. To cope with his pain and regret, he sleeps away the years and awakes in a new era with a powerful, ancient vampire who sets her sights on him.

Golden Shackles – Book 3: When the ancient queen, Sekhmet snatches up Adam, he is faced with a terrifying decision. To help aid her in her vile plans or dare to stand against her.

Plus 3 more segments!

Between the Trees

Kathy Moczerniak

https://www.lavishpublishing.com/authors/kathy-moczerniak/

A beautiful coming of age with a dark side that one teenager must fight to overcome…

Beyond Kathryn Lucas' first memory of her father's tree lay a dysfunctional path of violence, heartbreak, and secrets within a family severely entrenched in the vicious cycle of abuse. A lifetime of fear drives her from her home, and the teenage girl finds refuge with an aunt and uncle determined to protect their niece.

Distressing flashbacks unravel in Kathryn's fragile mind among the turmoil encircling her as she struggles through adolescence and descends into her pain-ridden past. When the summation of her unsettling memories allows the darkness to overtake her, she becomes desperate to unearth the light.

Inspired by a true story, Kathryn must hold on tightly to those who love her, searching for her place in a world threatening to break her as she fights to overcome life's betrayals before she is deprived of her future.